The Ashbee Cove

Monica Wade, Private Investigator, Mystery Series
CASE FILE: 001

by
Shea Adams

The Ashbee Cove Murders
by Shea Adams

Copyright 2019 by Shea Adams
All rights reserved

This edition published 2021 by
Papillon du Père Publishing
www.papillon-du-pere.com

Edited and compiled by
Jay Lewis Allchin, www.editing-store.com

Cover design by
Adam Tesla, Tesla Design Studio
www.fiverr.com/tesla_studio

This book is a work of fiction. Names, incidents, characters, or places are either drawn from the author's imagination or used fictitiously. Any resemblance to any persons, either living or dead, businesses and/or locations is coincidental.

No part of this book may be reproduced, scanned, or distributed in any printed or electronic form without the author's permission. Please do not participate or encourage piracy of copyrighted material in violation of the author's rights. Purchase and/or download only authorized editions.

Contents

Dedication	vii
Prologue	1
Chapter 1	3
Chapter 2	11
Chapter 3	21
Chapter 4	31
Chapter 5	53
Chapter 6	69
Chapter 7	91
Chapter 8	103
Chapter 9	115
Chapter 10	127
Chapter 11	141
Chapter 12	159
Chapter 13	169
Chapter 14	183
Chapter 15	195
Chapter 16	203
Chapter 17	211
Chapter 18	231
Epilogue	249
Afterword and thanks	251
About Shea Adams	253

Dedication

This book is dedicated to my family and to my many friends who have encouraged me to continue writing.

Prologue

Was it a crime of passion, a random killing, or a planned professional execution? Questions that started my investigation into the Ashbee Cove murders. Little did I know at the time that this case would lead me to the dark side of police corruption and the Irish mob, as well as the world of ancient antiquities and the legends & myths that make people commit the most heinous of crimes in the name of heritage and family.

Shea Adams

Chapter 1

It was a delightful morning in Malibu, California, sunny with temperatures expected to reach the mid-nineties.

Surfers were out catching that perfect wave, and a rainbow hue of umbrellas dotted the stretch of white sand in front of my bungalow. I had a delightful book, a steaming-hot cup of coffee, and I was looking forward to some quiet time.

Being a private investigator is one of those jobs that requires traveling, at times to other countries around the globe. I had just finished a case that had taken me to London for a few weeks. This kid fled the United States with a few pieces of his parents' collection of valuable art. Why? His parents caught him dealing drugs, cut him off financially, and he was pissed. Poor kid had no idea what was in store for him. His parents contacted me to retrieve the art and bring him home. I don't believe they wanted him back, but the art, *yes*. I flew to London, posed as a potential art buyer, convincing him that before I could consummate the deal, I needed him to fly back to the States with me and the art for authentication. His parents were waiting at LAX. They were getting their art back and the kid. Let's just say he was in for an extensive grounding, or worse.

The sun felt warm on my face as I perched myself on a comfortable lounger ready to dive into a book I had been trying to finish for a year. My serenity was about to change with a ring on my cell phone. The voice on the other end introduced himself as Steven Barnes.

"Yes, Mr. Barnes, what can I do for you?" My voice was reluctant. *Please don't let it be another case.*

"I got your number from a friend who said you might be able to help me."

"I see. What kind of help do you need?"

"I don't know where to start ..." I could feel the tenseness in his voice. "My brother Michael, his wife Sarah, and their two children, Abby and little Stevie, were ... murdered."

Hearing the word murder wasn't what I expected. "I'm sorry for your loss, Mr. Barnes. You do know I'm a private investigator; this sounds like something the police should handle."

"The police! They haven't come up with a single clue as to who the killer is. They've dropped the investigation!"

I could sense his desperation. "I'm sorry to hear that, but still, this isn't exactly my field of expertise."

"I don't care what it costs. I have nowhere else to turn. Please, Miss Wade. Could you just talk to the police and review their files? Maybe they missed something crucial."

I didn't want to take on another case so soon. Still, I felt compelled to say yes: a whole family murdered? For what reason?

"Where did the crimes happen, Mr. Barnes?"

"In Ashbee Cove. Their bodies were discovered aboard the Crystal Blue. Our family has had a home on Ashbee Lake for generations. We would spend every summer there when we were kids and, over the years, large family vacations together.

The Crystal Blue is a yacht we keep moored on Ashbee Lake, near the cabin. Michael and his family were there on vacation."

My gut was saying no, but my curiosity was saying yes. "Okay, Mr. Barnes, I'll see what I can do."

"Thank you, thank you, Miss Wade. I'll send you all the information by special courier, the keys to the cabin, where you can stay. Also the keys to the yacht. And your retainer will be included."

"Please remember, Mr. Barnes, I'm not making any promises."

"It's all I'm asking. I just want some kind of ... I need some closure. And the police aren't doing their job."

I had worked with police departments before, and the one thing they don't like is an investigator coming in and telling them how to do their job. But I also know that the police don't just throw a case into cold storage, especially the murders of an entire family. If Steven Barnes was to be believed, something didn't feel right. Probably why I found myself saying yes. Either I wasn't getting the complete story from Barnes or the Ashbee Cove Police department was less than competent. Looking at the files he was sending would give me clearer insight.

There is one person that will always give me their opinion. That friend everyone has who will tell you the truth no matter what. In my life, that person is Andy Weston. My forever, flamboyant gay friend that lives down the beach with his furry Shi-Tzu companion, Cloe. Andy keeps an eye on my bungalow, my mail, packages, and wine (I give him permission to indulge) whenever I am away on a case. I trust him with my life. I called Andy.

"Hi, sweetie. What are you and Cloe doing?"

"Watching those hard-body surfers. This time of the morning, their skin glistens." He laughed.

"Can you pull yourself away and come over? I need your opinion on something."

"My opinion? Must be something big! Sure, we'll come on over with a pitcher of my latest creation. Fruit & kale smoothie, plus some munchies—I'm sure you didn't eat anything this morning. This smoothie will keep you healthy. Right?

"Sounds good. See you in a bit."

One thing Andy always did was make sure my tummy was full, since he knows I don't cook, and he has a reputation as one of the best chefs on the beach.

My coffee was now cold but still tasted good with the addition of a little Bailey's Irish Cream. Making the three steps from the deck to the sand, I glanced down the beach in the direction Andy lived. Sure enough, here Andy came, sauntering across the sand with his chest puffed out, greeting everyone he saw with a jubilant "Hello! How are you today?"

"Hello, my queen!" I heard him calling out as he got closer. He was holding Cloe in her gold LeMay bag in one arm, balancing a pitcher his new smoothie for me to try on a golden platter full of goodies. He was, to say the least, quite the attraction. I met him as he approached, seeing that his hands were full.

"Can I help you with something?" I smiled.

"Grab Cloe, please."

I took Cloe and helped him negotiate the three steps up to the deck, then released Cloe out of her bag; she wiggled in my arms, licking my face and wagging her fluffy tail. "Nice to see you, too, Cloe." She got so excited she peed on my shirt.

Andy must have seen Cloe's little accident because he came from the kitchen with a wet towel. "Oops, sorry. You know how much she loves you."

I tried cleaning up my shirt but decided to change. When I came back, Cloe was sound asleep on the rug by the glass slider and Andy had our smoothies and food ready to enjoy. As he was pouring the green slush, he started laughing.

"Remember these glasses? We lifted them from the Rainbow Club."

"I do! That was the night you took me to that gay bar and I sat in the corner for hours watching as you eloquently worked the room."

"Now, let's not get pissy about it. I introduced you to Enrique, who was very attracted to you, if I recall!"

"No, not right. If I recall, Enrique wanted a *ménage à trois*."

Andy couldn't help but give up a burst of laughter, which was contagious. He filled our glasses, but not before rimming them with salt and lime. "So, what's up, dear queen?"

"I got a call this morning from a man who wants to hire me." Not making eye contact, I licked the salt from the glass.

"And that's unusual why?"

"It's something a little different from what I usually investigate."

"Quit beating around the bush and spit it out, girlfriend."

"In a nutshell, Steven Barnes's brother, wife, and two children were murdered."

Andy almost choked on his drink. "Murdered! The whole family? I hope you turned him down."

I said nothing.

"Damn it, Monica! Have you lost your fucking mind? Remember the last time you took on a case that involved dead bodies. You almost ended up as part of the body count."

"I know … but this is different."

"How different can *dead* be?"

"I just said I would consider it and ask a few questions. Barnes seems to think the police have just given up looking for the killer and dumped the file in the trash."

Andy refilled our drinks. "You, dear one, need a psychologist. Oh, wait. Don't you have a master's in this subject, along with speaking three languages fluently and hold a fifth-degree black belt? Does this sound like a good decision by someone so smart? I don't think so."

"Settle down, Andy."

"Crap, Monica. One of these days I'm going to get a call—not from you telling me you're on your way home, but from some stranger telling me you're *dead*!"

He was visibly upset, but he also knew me well enough that once my mind starts getting curious, there's no changing it.

"Mr. Barnes is sending me a package with as much information about the case as he was able to get. I'm going to review the case. That's all."

"My sweet ass. You'll take the case and probably get yourself killed. Am I in your will?" He stood up, came over, and gave me a big hug, then stood with his hands on his hips. "Okay, what do you need from me? Since you're going to play Wonder Woman."

I took his hand and looked up at his handsome face. "I just need you to be your supportive self and take care of my business like you always do. Let's not talk about it anymore today. Enjoy and relax with me. Okay?"

He settled in, and we changed the subject. The hours passed with our usual gossip and laughs and the evening ended with hugs from Andy and slobbery kisses from Cloe.

"I'll call you in the morning. I'll even make breakfast," I said.

"*You* call ... *I'll* make breakfast. I recall the last time you tried to make eggs. Those eggs, my dear Monica, were like chewing on a piece of rubber."

I watched Andy and Cloe stroll back to his place, stopping to greet people along the way. I knew deep inside that Andy was right about the case, but I needed to help Steven Barnes find closure. Plus, I was interested in why the police dropped this case.

That was very unusual with homicides.

Chapter 2

The next morning was overcast, and the Pacific Ocean was angry. Maybe a precursor to what lay ahead. I took a yellow notepad off my desk, poured a mug of coffee, and went out into the brisk ocean breeze to start a list of all the things I needed to do before leaving for Ashbee Cove. I had no worries about my personal affairs, because Andy would be here, regardless of his objection to me taking this case. List finished, I headed for a hot shower.

The warm water felt soothing as it massaged my muscles. I could faintly hear a voice from outside the bathroom door.

"Hello, hello? Where the hell are you?"

The glass shower door slid open.

I found myself standing stark naked, dripping wet in front of Andy, who was holding a steaming cup of coffee.

"Geez, Andy! Hand me a towel."

"Take it easy, girlfriend. I've seen it all before. Remember the time we both got drunk and went skinny-dipping at midnight under the moonlight?"

"Just give me the towel before I drip all over the floor, will you? And no, I remember nothing about that night." I laughed.

Andy handed me the towel as he propped himself up on the bathroom vanity.

"So, are you still going through with this madness, or have you come to your senses?"

"Out, out!"

He seemed a bit annoyed that I didn't want to talk to him wrapped in a bath towel, but a girl needs her personal space. Of course, Andy couldn't care less about me being naked. In fact, I could sit on his lap, naked as a jaybird, and it wouldn't phase him. He just wasn't attracted to women at all. Get a guy naked to sit on his lap, and things would change quickly. *Oh, I really don't want that picture stuck in my head.*

I dried off and took a sip of coffee before wrapping my hair in a towel and throwing on a robe, then joined Andy on the deck.

"Damn, it's cold out here!" he moaned, shivering on the deck.

"Then get your little butt inside, I'm starving."

"Oh, so I'm good enough to be your cook but not good enough to talk to you while you're naked?"

Always the joker.

It was a little selfish of me to take him for granted, I knew, but he was a damn good cook.

"What's the queen's pleasure this morning?" Andy asked as he put on an apron and tied it flamboyantly. "Never mind. How about I whip up a delicious Swiss-cheese and avocado omelet. Okay?"

He rummaged through the fridge, picking out the ingredients for what I knew would be worth devouring. I gave him a tight squeeze around the waist as he whipped the eggs.

"I don't want you to worry, Andy. This town where I'm going is small, and nothing like this has ever happened before. Pretty much me just going there and asking some questions."

Andy fixed us both a plate while I sat on the barstool at the counter. I took the towel off my head, shaking it dry.

"Please, no hair in the food ... When did this murder take place?"

"Six months ago."

"Shit, Monica. The killers could still be there! The murderer could be a cop or even the brother. I see it all the time on Law and Order."

He slid my omelet over to me. I inhaled the delicate aroma of the cheese and took a forkful. "Mmm, this is delicious. Thank you." I was trying to avoid his question.

"Where is this place, and what do you know so far?" Using a napkin, he wiped a string of cheese from my chin.

"As I said earlier, a place called Ashbee Cove, in the San Bernardino mountains. It happened aboard their yacht; they were killed with a gun and a knife."

"You do realize this sounds like a game of Clue and we're just missing the candlestick and butler?"

"It's not a game, Andy."

"Exactly my point. That's why I'm so worried. Whoever did this is dangerous and apparently crazy. Do you even know how to get to this Ashbee Cove?"

"Yep, googled it last night. Interstate 101 to the interchange, take the 210, then onto 60 East and follow the signs."

I finished eating, and Andy cleared the plates as I went to change.

When I came out, the sun was finally making an appearance, and Andy was sitting on one of the loungers, keeping a close watch on the surfers with my binoculars. I joined him.

"Do you know anything about this town?" Andy put down the binoculars.

"A little," I said. "It was a gold-mining town in the 1800s. A neighbor of Sam Brannon, who was living in San Francisco, prospected in that area and found gold. He returned to San Francisco to stake his claim and ran through the streets, proclaiming his gold find. Being a shrewd businessman and seeing an opportunity, Brannon moved himself and his family to Ashbee Cove. He became one of California's first millionaires by selling picks, shovels, dry goods, and gold-mining equipment, apparently.

"Sounds like a clever boy!"

"Yes, well, what with the influx of people arriving with gold fever, the town grew. Soon there was a bank, an assay office, and on every corner, an Irish saloon—"

"Serving up whiskey and beautiful women in the upstairs brothel?"

I laughed. "I think so, yes. And from current pictures, it hasn't changed much."

"Oh, doesn't it sound just charming and quaint? The perfect killing place." Andy shook his head.

The doorbell rang. "I'll get it." Andy jumped up to see who was at the door. He returned with a package. "Hope you don't mind, I signed your name. And this cute guy wearing tan shorts was looking me up and down. He didn't even notice I was a man, not a woman named Monica Wade." He gave me a wink.

"Leave the delivery guy alone. He's married and has five kids."

"Dear Lordy. Five? Well, he did look a little oversexed, but luscious just the same." Andy went into the house and came back with a letter opener. "Hurry up and open it!"

I was debating whether to open it in front of him. I knew it contained detailed information about the killings and probably some crime photos of the bodies. "No, I'll open it later. I just want to sit and enjoy the day with my best friend."

"I get it. You don't think I can handle what's inside?"

"Not at all." I changed the subject. "So, any new friends in your life?"

An effortless way to distract him was talking about his love life.

"Oh, yes! He's an actor. Just finished a movie."

"Would I have seen the movie he was in?"

"I doubt it. Besides when was the last time you saw a movie?"

"Is it a comedy, drama, what?"

"It's a remake of a classic, but the title was changed. The classic was 'Deep Throat.' The new title is 'Deep Throat—Only Bigger.'"

I started laughing. "Andy, you shit. That's a porno flick!"

"I know. Isn't it great to have a *big* movie star living on the same beach as us?"

"For you, yes; for me, no."

"Quit being a prude, Monica. Acting is an art form. And believe me, his part is worthy of an Oscar." Andy gave me a punch on my arm. "What do you need help with before you leave? Because I know you're going to trek through the wilderness to search for some deranged killer, aren't you?"

"Same as always, sweetie. Keep an eye on the place. I should only be gone for a few days."

"Okay, dear queen, but let's not forget the last time you said this, you were invisible for three months. Even though you taking this case is against my better judgment, yes I'll be here for you as always."

"I can pack myself, Andy. You don't need to help with that."

"Yes I do, Monica. I know everything that's in your closet, and what you have is unacceptable for going undercover as a mountain girl."

"Who said anything about being a mountain girl? I'm just going to ask some questions and tie up the loose ends Barnes is concerned about."

"So, smart-ass, you think arriving in a small town full of gold-mining lumberjacks, wearing designer jeans, silk shirts, and spiked heels is going to make you blend in when you're trying to get information from the cops? I don't think so."

I sighed. *He's right, damn it.* "Your suggestion, Mr. Armani?"

"It's all about a camp shirt, mountain boots, a bomber jacket, and an oversized sweater to hide those big boobs of yours. That flowing blonde mane goes into a ponytail, and nothing on your beautiful face but moisturizer and lip gloss. And I don't think showing up driving your Porsche is the best idea either. You can use my Jeep."

Again, he was right. A flashy single woman from Malibu would stand out, and that was not why I was going there. Still, I was not sure about leaving my car.

"Trust me, Monica. I'll look after Miss Candy; I'll guard your dear Porsche with my life." Andy placed his hand over his heart.

"I'm sure you will, Andy."

We worked in my closet, trying to find suitable outfits for my new mountain-girl look. I was surprised that I had some things that would fit the bill. Afterward, Andy left for home, and I would see him in the morning.

***

The bungalow was quiet, just leaving me and the package from Steven Barnes. It was late afternoon. I sat down at the table on the deck. Looking out over the massive body of blue ocean, I took a deep breath and opened the package.

Taking a sip of the vodka, I slid out the information along with a set of keys, clearly marked as cabin and yacht, and a small piece of paper that seemed to have a combination written on it. For being a murder of this magnitude, not much information was included. I inspected the disturbing photos of the crime scenes and the victims. The children had both been shot in the back of the head as they slept in their berths aboard the Crystal Blue. Michael Barnes was found in the captain's chair at the helm, also shot in the back of the head but his throat slashed, almost decapitating him. The body of Sarah, his wife, was discovered in the galley. She, too, was shot in the back of the head, with multiple stab wounds to the torso, and was, apparently, raped with a foreign object. I sat back in my chair, closed my eyes, wondering what kind of human being could inflict such deplorable acts on others. Next, I looked at what few reports there were from the police and the coroner's office, which told me nothing. No eyewitnesses, no forensics. How could a police department not find something—anything—to help them with their investigation? I was beginning to think Steven was right. The police had not done their job. *Why not?*

Words began crossing my mind like "vendetta," "professional hit." If it were just a random killing, clues would have been found at the scene. Why would this seemingly ordinary family on vacation at a cabin and yacht on a lake be targeted? I was starting to feel there was much more to this case than just a random killing. My curiosity heightened. This road trip might get a little bumpy.

I called Steven Barnes to accept the case formally. I would be leaving in the morning.

I had a sleepless night: images of this family had etched themselves in my mind. I woke up to the smell of fresh coffee and something sweet. Andy was in the kitchen. After showering, I joined him. "Morning, Andy. What smells so good?"

"Good morning to you, my crazy queen. Blueberry muffins, plus your favorite coffee."

"Coffee sounds good right now. Thanks, Andy. You don't know how much I appreciate all you do for me. Where's Cloe?" I sipped at the gorgeously dark, aromatic liquid before launching into a muffin. I sighed with pleasure.

"She's at the groomer but barked up a storm to tell you goodbye and to be safe."

"Very sweet of her." I smiled as I picked at another morsel.

"I see the smile, but I also see something hidden behind it, besides the muffin. What gives, Monica? You obviously didn't get much sleep last night."

"I looked at the files and photos. This information I got doesn't make any sense at all. The police, the coroner … Either they honestly haven't found any evidence or they are totally inept at their jobs."

"Are you all packed? Because I brought over a couple of things, you might need. A pair of mountain boots and my leather bomber jacket."

"Where did you get boots and a bomber jacket?"

"It's a long story and has to do with a guy and me on a Harley."

"Well, this is a story I'll be looking forward to hearing when I get back. You and a Harley, seriously?" I laughed, trying to remove a little tension.

He smiled back, coming up and giving me a big hug. "I filled the tank in the Jeep and checked all the fluids. Just remember it doesn't ride as smoothly as Candy. Are you ready?"

"Let's get this done. My luggage is in the bedroom. You'll be proud of me, Andy. It all fit in one suitcase. Well, and a carry bag."

Andy went to get my luggage while I put together my laptop and information from Steven into my briefcase. Lastly my .45 Glock, which I never leave home without, along with some extra ammo. I was waiting on the deck, taking one last long look at the Pacific, when Andy came over to where I was standing.

"Promise me you will not do anything stupid. And call me when you get there, okay?"

I kissed him on the cheek and gave him a reassuring hug. "I promise."

Andy carried my luggage out to the Jeep, which was in the driveway behind Candy.

"I'll talk to you soon, Andy."

Getting in the Jeep, I adjusted the mirrors and, as I waved and pulled out of the driveway, I heard Andy yell out, "Book 'em, Danno!"

Chapter 3

After an hour of winding my way through the maze of Los Angeles traffic, I finally turned off the Interstate and headed up into the San Bernardino Mountains. I estimated my driving time would be around four to five hours. The two-lane road in front of me and the blackened sky of smog hovering over the Los Angeles basin behind me, I was on my way. It was undoubtedly beautiful and serene once the altitude changed. The rolling hills, covered in wild mustard and lavender, filled the air with aromatic cleanliness. My mind was surprisingly relaxed until I looked at the gas gauge.

Damn, this Jeep gets horrible mileage. Well, I needed to find a station. Ah, my lucky day: a shredded sign reading "REDS, next gas for seventy miles." Exiting the main road, I traveled for the next three miles on a potholed, rollercoaster two-lane road. I've always enjoyed riding in Jeeps, but the suspension sucks, and I found myself bouncing around like a ping-pong ball.

Luckily, I soon spotted REDS, a big red barn-like building with one gas pump, its sign on the pump: "Pump first, pay after." I felt like I had been catapulted into a time warp or the Ozarks. I filled the tank and started inside to pay the cashier, trying to avoid the holes filled with muddy water. Opening a creaky screen door, I knew that I had indeed stepped back in time. To my left was a small old-fashioned soda fountain with four stools, each with chrome bases and red leather seats. Racks of snacks were scattered about the small room, a large cold box with a neon sign hanging unevenly on a chain, proclaiming "Beer and Bait." Making my way to the counter, I didn't see anyone, at first, until a thin man dressed in dirty overalls stepped through a small door. Another sign hung above, also unevenly on a chain, read "Cowgirls and Cowboys," which, I assumed, was a shared restroom. From the awful smell that was following the guy, I would rather pee on the side of the road than walk through that door.

"What can I do you for, Missy?" His smile exposed a huge gap of missing front teeth.

"I just filled up with gas. How much do I owe you?"

Taking out a #2 pencil, he jotted down a number on a yellow sticky note. It read $87.28. *What the ...?* I didn't want to buy the place!

"Is this the correct amount, sir? It seems rather expensive for a tank of gas."

"Well, pretty lady, I am really good with numbers."

I knew this would not be a conversation I was going to win. "Do you take credit cards or debit?"

"Nope. Daddy always said only to take cash. It's store policy."

"Do you have change for a hundred?"

Looking at me with his vacant tooth smile, he said. "Most likely." He opened up a dirty white-stained envelope he pulled from a drawer under the old rusty cash register. "You gave me a hundred-dollar bill, so I owe you how much?" He started to hand me the stack of dirty money.

"No, that's fine. You keep the change."

"Okay," he said, stuffing the hundred-dollar bill in his pocket.

"You must have been here for a long time. How did this place get its name?" I was about to regret my nosiness.

"Been here since I was born. I worked with my mommy and daddy; that's how I learned the business. They're gone now, God rest their souls. Some bad guys came in one afternoon and shot them both dead. They didn't get me because I ran and hid in the goat pen."

"Oh, I'm sorry for your loss." I turned and started to leave.

"This here place used to be called Little Reds, but the "little" fell off that sign out front during a storm. Mommy had red hair, and she was Irish; my daddy was full-blood Paiute Indian. All my kin are buried out back under that goat shit."

"I better get back on the road. It was interesting talking with you. Oh, by the way. How much further is Ashbee Cove?"

"Not far. You gonna do some fishing? Because I got some good fat worms in that cold box with the beer."

"No fishing, just visiting. But thanks, anyway."

My steps increased in speed as I walked through the creaky screen door until I reached the Jeep, thinking to myself that this would be the guy who puts back in his dentures, puts on a leather coat, gets into his new Cadillac, and heads to the bank, all the time muttering to himself "Stupid flatlanders."

Finding my way back to the main road, I headed even further up the mountain. My guess was I had driven up to about 3,500 feet elevation. I could see the landscape changing from scrub oaks to pine trees and redwoods. I recalled from my research that Ashbee Cove was at about five thousand feet or so. Putting the Jeep into a lower gear, I drove the windy road that curved through the mountains like a giant python.

Finally, a sign! "Ashbee Cove – Elevation 5000 ft. – Population 1,050."

The town was quaint, as I expected from the pictures, sporting an appearance of the old gold-mining era, with raised wooden walkways and rustic brick buildings flanking the main street. Even old-fashioned "hitching posts" for you to tie up your horse while taking care of business in town. Ashbee Cove, because of its historical background, had become an attractive place for tourists, who enjoyed shopping in the charming boutiques or camping near Lake Ashbee. Motor crafts could cruise the lake, at five mph, with speedboats and water skiing prohibited.

Steven Barnes had included a map, marking the location of the cabin, but it was in my bag, in the back of the Jeep. I pulled into the first horizontal parking space I could find, right in front of a place called "Flynn's Pub." Finding the map in my bag, I had just started to unfold it when I felt a tap on my shoulder.

"Are you lost, Miss?"

My body jolted. There he stood: a tall, tan, well-built, gorgeous blue-eyed man, with a smile that could lighten up the darkest night sky.

"Are you ...? Lost?"

I stammered to find my voice. "J-just a little lost. I'm on my way to the erm, Barnes place. Do you know it?"

He approached closer. "Everyone knows the Barnes lake home. Just follow the main street out of town, take a left, and follow the road around the lake. Can't miss it. Are you a friend of the family?"

Should I tell this stranger I'm a PI or tell a lie? I decided a little white lie was acceptable. "I'm the family's attorney."

"The town is still in shock over the deaths of Michael Barnes and his family. Is that why you're here?"

I just recreated myself, so I needed to come up with something that would make sense. "My name is Christy Manning, and yes, I'm here to tie up some loose ends for Steven Barnes. And you are, sir?" At that moment, his beeper went off.

"Sorry, I need to get back to work. Nice meeting you, Miss Manning. Maybe I'll see you around. How long are you staying?" He turned, speaking as he walked away, giving me no time to answer. But yes, I also hoped to see *him* again. Few men can make my blood pressure rise.

I folded the map, got back in the Jeep, and followed this stranger's instructions. Lake Ashbee was beautiful, quiet—not a place one would think that just months ago, four individuals were brutally murdered. Finally, I spotted a sign that read "Camp Barnes." There it stood at the end of the road, sitting on the water's edge: the redwood log cabin standing majestically overlooking the lake, with the Crystal Blue docked nearby. The perfect cabin, perfect location, where anyone would love to spend time. But an unlikely place for mass murder.

This fantastic cabin would be my temporary home for a few days. Maybe the walls would speak to me and give me a direction of where to start. Well, stranger things had happened to me before. Like a case where I was hired to find a child who had been kidnapped by the biological father and taken across the border to a small village in Mexico. The town had limited resources, like police, so I was on my own. I speak Spanish fluently, as well as some French, Japanese, and Italian, so communicating with the township wasn't hard, but there was little to go on. I searched for a week with no success. One day, after leaving a local Bodega, heading back to my hotel, I stumbled on the uneven pavement, dropping my bag of fresh fruit. As I was putting my now bruised apples and bananas back in the bag, I looked up and noticed some bright-yellow daisy plants on the balcony of a ramshackle home just across the street. In that instant, I knew that was where the child was being held. How did I know that?

Putting two and two together, the father was a landscaper, and the plants just looked out of place. I contacted the police and, after convincing them that I knew where the child was, they agreed to accompany me to the home. I was able to return the child to the mother, and the father was extradited back to the United States to face kidnapping charges.

I began unloading the Jeep, putting all my luggage and equipment onto the redwood porch, which encircled the entire cabin.

Footsteps ... a voice was approaching me from behind.

Instinctively, I reached under the front seat of the Jeep for my Glock.

"Hello."

Pulling back the slide, I turned and pointed in the direction of the voice. I don't know who was more surprised! Me or the old man with a cane who was looking down the barrel of my gun.

"Whoa, little lady! Mind pointing that in another direction. I'm Charlie Towne, your neighbor, up the road. I was taking my daily walk and noticed a strange vehicle here at the Barnes place."

"I'm sorry, sir. You ... startled me." I put my gun on the seat of the Jeep.

Tapping his cane on the ground, he asked, "Are you a relative?"

"No, sir. Just a friend here to get some loose ends tied up for the family."

"So tragic about the family being killed. Nothing like this has ever happened in Ashbee Cove before. Say, that's a big gun for such a little lady. Sure, you're not a thief?"

I smiled sweetly. "I assure you that I have permission from Steven Barnes to be here."

He nodded. "Well, if you need anything, I'm just up the road. And please don't call me 'sir.' Name's Charlie. The only people that called me 'sir' were those snot-nosed rich kids that I trained at the military academy."

"Are you a veteran?"

He looked at me with a grin. "Yep, Special Forces."

"Well, I thank you for your service, Mr. Towne ... I mean, Charlie." The respect I had for our military and veterans was a passion of mine. When I had extra time, I would volunteer at the local veterans' hospital; I just hated the way our government treated our vets. Shameful.

"Thank you kindly. I was proud to serve. You take care. I'm sure I'll see you again. Have a lovely day." He started to walk back down the drive.

He seemed harmless enough, but still, I knew that anyone and everyone here could be possible suspects.

Taking a deep breath, inhaling the fresh air, I unlocked the front door. This was an incredible cabin! Thirty-foot open-beamed ceilings, a massive stone fireplace, overstuffed leather furniture, and floor-to-ceiling windows that overlooked the lake. Off the main room, I found a library, with another fireplace and wall-to-wall bookshelves filled with literary masterpieces. I ran my hand gently across some of the spines of Dickens after Dickens, Hardy, Melville, the Bard, of course. The kitchen was large, fully equipped with all stainless-steel appliances. There were three good-sized bedrooms, each with a private full bath, in addition to the master bedroom, which was far from average. Certain words came to mind: wealth, opulence. But it was comfy, too.

I started unpacking, taking one of the bedrooms in the front of the house rather than the master suite. I set up my laptop on the large oak desk in the library. Well, it looked out over the lake, so who wasn't going to set up an office there? Not to mention that, in one corner, was a fully stocked bar, complete with bar stools, that looked like it had been hand-carved from rich mahogany.

I walked out onto the front porch, sitting down in one of the hand-carved log chairs that faced the water. The cabin sat oddly on the property, which encompassed the whole north side of the lake. A circle driveway entrance to the north and, to the south, lay the Crystal Blue. Extensive decking, an outside kitchen, a fire pit for those chilly evenings, and a diving dock. To the back of the property were tennis, basketball, and Bocce Ball courts. Different sheds sat scattered about, which I assumed were for property equipment.

The surroundings were eerily quiet, with just the sound of a breeze rustling through the giant redwoods and pines. There was no one on the lake, which surprised me with all the tourists I had seen on my way through town. Tomorrow I would introduce myself to Police Chief Cullen Armstrong and County Coroner Trevor Bowen. For now, it was all about clearing my mind and focusing on the tasks at hand. Well, that and simply soaking in the peace.

Ahh, I could get used to this.

Shea Adams

Chapter 4

I slept surprisingly well, considering I was in a strange place, but then I was used to that. Rarely home anymore, I needed to consider making this my last case for a while, to slow down a little ... get a life.

There was a crisp breeze filtering through the bedroom window. The sheer drapes were dancing to the whisper of the wind, and the smell of the redwoods was refreshing. Getting up, I dressed and went to the kitchen to make coffee. Steven had taken a considerable amount of liberty in assuming I would take the case, even making sure the cabin was well stocked with everything I would need. I poured a mug of coffee, then entered the library, sat at the desk, and opened the files to read about the people I would be meeting with this afternoon.

Chief Cullen Armstrong: sixty-two years old, widowed, no children, transferred from Boston to Ashbee Cove ten years ago. Made chief after the previous chief of police died. No information included as to how he died. I hoped it was from natural causes.

Trevor Bowen: fifty years old, single, never married, no children. A gifted individual who graduated from high school at age sixteen attended Stanford University, where he received his master's and Ph.D. in forensic science. Came to Ashbee Cove eight years ago from San Francisco, where he was chief medical examiner, practicing forensic pathology for the City and County of San Francisco.

Hmm, no explanation as to why he left the city.

How was I going to approach these two men without raising suspicion that I was investigating the murders? I had already told one lie to the man who helped me with directions. I smiled and gazed out the window, recalling those intense eyes.

Not now, Monica.

My issue at hand was how to handle grilling a police department like a cheese sandwich. Cooperation is often not readily forthcoming. Impugning the integrity of the coroner's office is not so smart either. So my ruse of being Attorney Christy Manning, handling legal matters for the family, would be my cover.

It was still early, the lake beckoning me to take a dip before heading into town. One problem, though: Andy forgot to pack my swimsuit. The lake was deserted, probably no harm in taking a quick dip without proper attire, right? At forty-seven years old, and a birthday just around the corner, my body still looked good. Butt was tight, boobs still perky, and my small waist hadn't changed since high school. My naked reflection in the mirror was not repulsive, or at least I didn't think so.

Stepping onto the diving deck, I dropped the towel and dove into the blue water. I swam over to where the Crystal Blue was berthed. She was a magnificent yacht, but out of place on a lake. I didn't feel it was the right time for me to go aboard so, instead, I stepped onto the running board and dove back into the water. As I pushed off the bottom of the lake, my foot caught on something, which felt sharp and jagged. I shouldn't be surprised how much junk might be sitting on the bottom. As I broke the surface of the water, I saw a small boat with two men, just sitting idle in the water, the older gentlemen staring at me.

"What are you two staring at?" I tried to keep my naked body hidden by treading water.

"Sorry, Miss. We thought you were a mermaid." They both laughed.

"Really. Are there mermaids in this lake? Have you ever seen one before?" I jabbed.

"Now that you mention it, nope. I think you're the first one we've seen." One of them took off his baseball hat and scratched his head.

"I'm not a fucking mermaid, guys. Could you just leave so I can finish my swim?"

"You don't have to get nasty, Miss Mermaid. Nice talking to you." With that said, they motored towards the South Shore.

Waiting until they were out of sight, I stepped back onto the diving deck and wrapped myself up in my towel. As I was drying off, I looked down and saw blood oozing from my foot. *What the hell? Great, just what I don't need. Damn it!*

I hobbled over to a deck chair, trying to wipe the blood away so I could examine my foot. There was about a two-inch cut on the side. I dropped the towel and wrapped it around my foot, limping into the house. There must be a first-aid kit around here somewhere. I found one in the kitchen pantry, which had everything I needed: gauze, disinfectant, and tape. I proceeded to clean up my foot, and it didn't appear to be as deep as I thought, once I cleared away all the blood. But it was throbbing like crazy.

Now what? I had already made plans to meet with the chief and coroner, but not barefooted. I dug out my Extra Strength Tylenol from my bag. I put on a pair of blue jeans and a white cotton shirt, but no way in hell a shoe was going on this foot. The best thing was just to wear flip-flops. *Wonder what I cut my foot on?* Thank goodness it was my left foot, but still, it would be challenging using a stick shift.

Getting myself comfortable in the driver's seat of the Jeep was challenging but not as complicated as I thought it would be. The drive into town wasn't easy. With every turn on the winding road, every chug hole I hit sent shooting pains from my foot to my head.

Once in town, the only parking space available was across the street from the police station, in front of the coroner's office. Gently putting my foot onto the asphalt, I tried walking as normally as possible, but I looked ridiculous. I limped up the brick steps of the Ashbee PD and through the heavy wooden doors. The inside was grand in every sense of the word. Shiny mosaic tile flooring, offices lined each side of the main floor, with block print letters as to who was behind the frosted-glass doors. In the middle of the room, a horseshoe-shaped reception desk, flanked by large staircases, leading to the second floor. A young freckled-faced redhead was behind the counter, talking on the phone. She looked up as I approached.

With a soft voice and a delicate smile, she purred, "Oh, honey, you must be in the wrong place. The emergency clinic is across the street."

Naturally, she would think this since I was barely walking and had "pain" written all over my face. "Thank you, but I'm here to see Chief Armstrong."

She blushed at her assumption. "I'm sorry; it was just that you look hurt."

"Just a little cut on my foot. Is the chief available?"

She pushed the intercom button. "Chief Armstrong, there's someone here to see you."

Looking at me, she whispered, "What's your name?"

"Attorney Christy Manning. I'm here at the request of Steven Barnes."

"Attorney Christy Manning, sir. Steven Barnes sent her."

"I'll be right out."

A few minutes later, the chief came into the foyer. "Miss Manning. I'm Chief Cullen Armstrong. What can I do for you?" He extended his hand, professional.

I gripped his hand with a firm handshake. Most men are surprised when a woman shakes her hand with strength. It shows we're sure of ourselves, implanting into their male ego that they should take us seriously. "I'm the attorney for the Barnes estate. There are just a few questions I have to ask and get some copies of the reports regarding the case."

He looked down at my foot. "Can you walk okay? We can talk in my office." He graciously took my arm, leading me a few feet past the redhead to his office.

"Please, have a seat. Can I get you anything? Water? Coffee?"

"No, thank you, sir."

"What happened to your foot, if you don't mind me asking?"

"Just a stupid accident."

He leaned back in his chair, placing his arms behind his head. "So, what can I do to help the Barnes family, Miss Manning?"

"The estate needs some paperwork involving the deaths of Michael and his family. Police reports, evidence lists, and crime photos."

"Excuse me, Miss Manning, but those records are confidential. Why would the estate need them?"

"As the attorney for the Barnes family, some documents need to be completed before any funds are allocated."

"Did Michael leave behind a large estate? I thought all the boys had was the family house and their own investment business."

"All I can tell you, Chief, is that they are relevant to the estate. As their attorney, Steven gave me the task of getting this information together. I have a request from Steven himself, giving me the authority to act on his behalf. Would you like to see it, sir?" I was so bluffing through this whole scenario.

36

"That's quite all right, Miss Manning. If Steven needs them, I'm sure there's a reason. I'll have Debbie, our receptionist, make you copies."

"Can I ask you a personal question, Chief? Why has the case been closed? I would assume a murder of this magnitude, and given the Barnes name and long history in the community, your department would be moving heaven and earth to find the killer."

I could tell from the look on Armstrong's face that I had stepped into forbidden water. He stared at me, sternly. "I assure you, Miss Manning. This department has done everything humanly possible to uncover any clues leading to the killer and why the family was murdered. Now, if you will excuse me, I have a meeting to attend."

I got up from my chair. "I appreciate your time, Chief, and thank you for getting those records together for me. I'm sure Steven appreciates your cooperation."

"If there's anything else I can do to help Steven Barnes, please have him give me a call." I took that little barb to mean, *Don't come back in my office again.*

"Oh, Miss Manning. Here are copies of the files you wanted on the Barnes murder." Debbie, the receptionist, caught me just as I was leaving the building.

I took the box of files, which contained more than I expected. "Thanks, Debbie."

"Would you like me to carry those to the car for you?" she asked with a smile.

"Thank you, but I think I can make it." She smiled again and waved bye as I walked down the steps.

I looked across the street, wondering if making a friendly call on the coroner's office was such a good idea after the reception I got from Chief Armstrong. Might as well get it over with since the Jeep was parked right in front. Easy in and easy out.

The building was like most of the others on Main Street: old brick but surrounded by lush gardens on either side, a white gazebo to the left with a rose garden and a flowing fountain.

What a peaceful place to be, I thought. If indeed you were called into the morgue to identify the body of a loved one. I'm sure it wasn't easy for Steven Barnes. He would have had to identify not just his brother but his niece, nephew, and Michael's wife, Sarah.

I entered through the large glass doors. Unlike the police foyer, there was no one attending a reception desk. Two long hallways ran off either side of the empty reception desk. I just took a guess and started walking down the sterile hallway to my right. It was eerily quiet, with a feeling of pure coldness, much in contrast to the outside's surrounding gardens. I continued a short distance, when a male voice echoed through the silence. "Miss Manning?"

Now, there were only three people in Ashbee Cove that know I'm Christy Manning: me, the chief, and the cute guy I met on the street who helped me with directions to the Barnes cabin. I turned, and there he was, the handsome man with a beeper.

"Hi. Aren't you the Good Samaritan who helped me yesterday?" I smiled.

He didn't answer the question, just looked down at my foot. "Only in town one day and you're already injured?"

"Just a cut on my foot. I'm alright." I hoped to hell that the pain wasn't showing on my face.

"It doesn't look fine to me. My office is right down the hall. I can look at it for you."

"No that's okay. I'm here to see a Mr. Trevor Bowen, the coroner. Could you direct me to his office, please?"

"I can do better than that. I'll show you to his office; I'm sure he's close by."

"Thank you." I couldn't help but catch a whiff of his cologne as he escorted me to Bowen's office. It had a distinctive aroma of orange blossom, jasmine, tiaré blossom, patchouli, ylang-ylang, iris, vanilla, and sandalwood. How did I know this? The name of the cologne is Hermes 24 Faubourg; it sells for fifteen hundred dollars an ounce and trades exclusively in the more elegant men's boutique stores in Paris, France.

I was handling a case a couple of years ago. I was hired to retrieve a priceless diamond ring that was stolen from a wealthy couple visiting the United States from France. After a few weeks of trying to track down leads Stateside, the clues led me to Paris. Unfortunately, it was not a happy ending for the thief, who turned out to be their personal valet. Yep, the butler did it. The gentleman who hired me wore this fragrance; I liked it so much he gave me a bottle. Do I wear it? No, but on occasions, I do open the bottle and savor the aroma or dab a little behind my knee, sometimes a few precious drops into my bubble bath. It's very intoxicating. And sexy as hell.

"Please have a seat, Miss Manning." He pulled out my chair, seating himself behind a desk, piled with paperwork.

I peeked over the stack of loose papers and started laughing. "Ah, Trevor Bowen, I presume."

"Well, I did say he was close by. So, what do I owe the pleasure of seeing you again?"

Deep breath, Monica. "I'm here at the request of Steven Barnes and am the attorney for the estate. He asked me to look at all the files regarding the death of his brother Michael and his family."

"I see." He was questioning my being there, but the ruse had to seem professional.

"I must be honest with you, Miss Manning. The chief called me and said you were on your way over."

"Good. Then I won't have to repeat myself." I gave him a smile, tinged with pain.

"I already took the liberty of putting everything I thought you might need together." Shuffling the stack of papers on his desk, he pulled out four file folders.

I get a box from the chief but only four folders from the coroner. "Is this it?" I raised one eyebrow to show my concern.

"I'm afraid so. Each folder contains all the autopsy reports on each victim."

"I'm still somewhat confused as to why this case was declared closed."

"To tell you the truth, there was nothing to find. I did a thorough investigation. No clues left behind. No forensics. Whoever committed the murders did a decent job of covering their tracks. Everything is in the files. As far as the case's status, that's the chief's call."

"I'm sure this will be okay with Steven. Thank you, Mr. Bowen."

"Of course. You seem to be in a lot of pain, Miss Manning. Why don't you let me write you a prescription for the pain and an antibiotic? You don't want that infected."

"You can write scripts for a perfect stranger?" I asked with a smile of relief.

"All kinds of strangers, in fact." He smiled. "And, yes, I'm a doctor. Contrary to what most people think, I don't *just* cut open dead bodies." He pointed to one of the many diplomas on his wall.

"Okay, you're the doctor." I watched as he pulled a script pad from his desk. As he was writing, I glanced at the many other diplomas he had displayed in his office. One picture, of what I assumed was a local landscape, but no photos of family or even a girlfriend. Could it be this Adonis of a man was single?

After he had finished writing, he stood and came around the desk to my chair, putting his hand on my shoulder as he gave me the script. "This will help."

"Thank you. I'm sure it will. The pain seems to be getting worse." Again, I smiled with grimacing pain.

"Tell you what. I'll fill the prescription for you at the hospital pharmacy and bring it to you this afternoon. You don't need to be walking around. That foot needs to be elevated."

"I don't want to bother you, Mr. Bowen." Of course, I wanted him. To "bother" me, I mean. To see that gorgeous face again.

"It's no trouble. I'll get off a little early, so it's great for me. You're at the Barnes cabin, right?

"That's right." Did he forget that I asked him directions? I had to chuckle.

He helped me up from the chair, putting his hand around my waist to steady me. We walked down the hallway, he opened the door, and escorted me to the Jeep, opening the door and helping me inside. I took the files he handed me and put them in the passenger seat.

"Are you sure you're okay to drive?"

"I'll be fine. And thank you again."

"Okay then, I'll see you in a couple of hours with some feel-good pills," he said with a flip sense of humor.

I backed out onto Main Street, then remembered I needed to stop at the little market I saw on my way into town. Thank goodness it was small and not a Wal-Mart superstore. I picked up what I needed, plus some lovely ripe tomatoes, fresh basil, Feta cheese, and French bread. You guessed it. Maybe some nice bruschetta would complement the evening, paired with some vintage wine from the wine cabinet behind the bar. Of course, it was possible he would just drop off the pills on the front porch and leave. My thoughts were that I would like to get to know him better. Keeping my mind focused on the reason I was in Ashbee Cove, maybe I could sugar and spice some more information out of him other than what he gave me in four file folders.

It would be a few hours before Mr. Bowen would arrive, giving me time for a quick shower and to put together the bruschetta, which I managed with not a lot of time to spare. I heard a vehicle coming up the driveway. I peeked through the shades. He wasn't wearing his white lab coat, instead had on jeans and a tight-fitting t-shirt. And from the outline underneath those clothes, he was in great shape.

I opened the door to greet him.

"Come in, Doctor Bowen." He was holding a small white bag in one hand.

"How's the pain?" he asked as he walked into the living room, setting the bag on the mahogany coffee table in front of the overstuffed leather couch, where he noticed my half-sipped glass of wine.

"I see you've started your own self-medication."

"Just a sip. I'm not much on taking pills." I sat down on the couch.

He sat down beside me. "Let me look at that foot." Sitting one of the throw pillows on the table, he gently lifted my leg, resting my foot on the pillow.

All that kept going through my mind was, did I remember to shave my legs? Yes, I did.

"The cut isn't that bad. It was just such a stupid accident."

"Let's see what's under that bandage." He started unwrapping my not-so-expert job of bandaging.

"Tell me, Doctor Bowen, do you think feel-good pills and wine isn't such a good idea?" I said, smiling as I reached for my glass of wine from the coffee table.

He continued to unwrap my foot. "No, it's not the best idea."

"As I said, I'm not much on taking pills, really, and the wine is helping with the pain." My eyes met his.

"Then I, as your doctor, suggest you have another glass." He was now looking at the cut on my foot. "Hmm. You did a suitable job taking care of this cut."

"Thank you, Doc." I was going for cute; not sure if he appreciated my sense of humor, though.

"It doesn't appear to be infected, but you should still take the antibiotics just in case. As for the pain, everyone has their own threshold of tolerance, so I'll let you decide if you need to take them. The ones I brought you aren't very strong, but they'll ease the throbbing and muscle aches."

I took my leg off the pillow. "Can I get you something to drink, Doc?"

He stood up, facing me. "Since I'm officially off doctor duty, sure. Do you have any Scotch?"

"I think there's a bottle behind the bar in the library." I started to get up.

"Just sit. I can get it." He walked straight into the library. How did he know where it was?

He came back with his glass of Scotch. "Since you know where the library is, you must have been here before?"

"I have. Michael and Sarah were big supporters of Ashbee Cove and donated kindly to many of the charity events we had. Especially if they involved the medical needs of the community. In fact, they gave the town the money to build the hospital. It's small but adequate for a small town's needs. Plus, they were very generous in financing some of the equipment I needed to upgrade the coroner's office."

"They must have cared very much about Ashbee Cove." I could tell he was a compassionate man. He sat beside me swirling the ice in his glass of Scotch. When he looked at me, there were tears in his eyes.

"Yes, they did. The Barnes family has been a part of Ashbee from its beginnings. That's what's so hard to fathom ... why the hell someone would kill them. It just doesn't make any sense."

I put my hand on his leg, lightly. "It must have been hard for you doing the autopsies on their bodies, especially the children." I felt this need inside of me to comfort him.

He looked at me and smiled. "One of the hardest things I've ever had to do."

I needed to change the subject to something a little less traumatic. "I made some bruschetta. Are you hungry?"

"Not really." He still looked sadly into his Scotch.

"Still, you must try some. I make a mean bruschetta." I started to get up from the couch.

He stopped me, putting his hand in mine. "We need to get two things clear: you need to call me Trevor. And I know where the kitchen is. I'll get the bruschetta; you just sit and relax. Doctor's orders."

"It's already on the tray in the kitchen, Doc ... I mean, Trevor."

With that said, he walked into the kitchen, returning a moment later with the bruschetta. He set the tray on the table.

"This looks good." He took one, placing it on a napkin before taking a small bite.

I watched as he enjoyed the one thing I knew how to prepare, and that's because Andy had shown me repeatedly the proper way to put together a tempting bruschetta.

He noticed my wine glass was empty. "More wine?"

"Please. The bottle's on the bar. Thanks." I liked this man and his attention.

"So, Miss Manning. Tell me how you got this nasty cut on your foot."

"Only if you call me Christy," I said as he filled my glass.

He smiled. "Christy, how did you do this?"

"Long story short. When I got here, the lake looked very inviting, so I decided to take a swim. I dove in, and when I pushed off the bottom, I felt something sharp scrape my foot. When I got out of the water and onto the deck, it was bleeding. End of story."

He started to chuckle. "Now, don't get upset when I ask you this, but are you the mermaid that was swimming naked in the lake?"

I was shocked that he asked that question. How did he know? "Yes, I was ... well, erm, naked. How—"

"Two of my friends told me a story about when they were fishing on the lake. They swore up and down they saw a mermaid. Guess they were right."

I could feel the tension leave the room. Trevor's laughter was contagious. "Oh, stop laughing! It was pretty embarrassing, and those two guys wouldn't leave, so I had to tread water for like five minutes."

"You're lucky they left. Don't know if I would have been able to leave such a beautiful mermaid behind."

Could this conversation be getting a little too personal? "I'm flattered, Trevor. I think."

"I have some bandages in my SUV. I need to wrap that foot again." He walked out to his Hummer, returning with a first-aid kit, much better stocked than the one I found in the cabin.

Again, he lifted my leg onto the pillow. Carefully, gently rubbing the antibiotic cream on the cut and handling the gauze. Like the pro he was, he wrapped my foot. "How does that feel, Christy? Too tight?"

"No, it's great. Thank you." Not the most romantic setting, having a handsome man wrap your foot, but erotic—in a friendly way.

The sky was beginning to dim, the night air cool. "Trevor, would you like to go sit outside? The view of the lake from the deck is beautiful."

"Sounds good." He helped me up from the couch. "Can you walk okay?"

"Yep. I have a great doctor." He gave me that pearly-white smile as he touched my shoulder.

"I'll refresh our drinks and meet you on the deck." He picked up our glasses and headed to the bar as I limped out to the deck. The sun was just beginning to set; it was breathtaking. Almost as good as the sunsets on the beach.

Trevor joined me on the deck. "It *is* beautiful."

"For sure." I blushed.

"I mean the other scenery." He came over where I was sitting, sat our drinks on the table, then took my hand.

"There's something I need to tell you, Christy." He looked so sweet and innocent.

Being responsive, I put my hand on his. "What is it, Trevor?"

"I don't mean to be forward, but from the first time I saw you yesterday on Main Street, looking at your map, I knew I wanted to see you again. And, as fate would have it, you walked into my office, and I was once again taken back at the sight of you."

"Wow. I don't know what to say." Now my mind was reeling, like a fisherman bringing in a big one. Perhaps that's just what I was doing.

"Don't say anything. I just wanted you to know that you made quite an impression on me. Been a long time since these types of feelings have surfaced. Please don't be embarrassed."

"I'm not embarrassed ... In fact, I'll admit that I hoped to see you again, as well." Should I tell him the truth, that I'm not Christy Manning, attorney for the Barnes estate? What if he was the killer? I didn't want to keep my identity a secret from him, didn't want this lie to be something that might put a barrier between us.

"Then you won't mind if I kiss you?" He pulled his chair closer to me, taking my face in his strong hands. I could feel his breath on my cheek. My heart was throbbing out of my chest.

I pushed him away. "Wait, Trevor. I need to tell you something."

He looked at me. "You're going to say that you aren't Christy Manning the attorney, but that your real name is Monica Wade, a private investigator."

I stood up, the pain rushing to my head. "How did you know?"

He stood to face me. "Don't get upset, please. Steven called me this afternoon after you left my office. You forget that he and I go back a long way. He just wanted to confide in me that he sent an investigator to consider the deaths of his brother and family. It doesn't matter. I understand why Steven needs closure. I told him I would help you any way I can."

"Oh, I see. Well, I'm sorry for trying to deceive you, Trevor. I didn't want anyone to know that I was investigating the murders."

Without speaking another word, he stood, wrapped an arm gently around me, and passionately kissed me. It seemed to last forever as my body went limp. I returned the passion. Then we just held each other for a few moments.

"Where do we go from here, Monica?"

"What do you mean by 'we'?" I was still in his embrace.

"I want to help find who killed the Barnes family as much as you do. Does that surprise you?"

"This is awkward, Trevor. You're the coroner, and what you handed me today, four small files, doesn't help me much."

We both sat back down, but he continued to hold my hand. "Those aren't all the files."

"I don't understand." What was he trying to tell me?

"I think I know who killed them, but, really, I found no evidence or forensics to back up my theory."

"What theory?"

"It's going to sound crazy, but I think Chief Armstrong and his department are covering up something."

I regarded him, forcing my passion to drop away. He seemed sincere: his tone, his face.

"Seriously, you think the police had something to do with this? That's a little out there, even for a PI."

"It's crazy, I know. But there are too many things that don't back up my findings," he insisted.

"You're telling me there was evidence left behind and that the chief didn't act on it?"

"Exactly. By the time I arrived at the scene, there were deputies on the yacht all over the place. They were combing the grounds. That isn't a police procedure. The scene should have been shut down tight until I got there, but it wasn't. They had touched everything and removed evidence that might have been crucial to identifying the killer. It was all tainted, and the chain of evidence was broken. Even if they arrested someone, it wouldn't have held up in court. It was like it was being tampered with on purpose."

"Did you talk to the chief about it? The way the investigation was handled and your concerns?"

"Of course not. You don't question Chief Armstrong. He's got a firm hold on this town. Most people here are afraid of him."

"You do know how absurd this sounds, Trevor?" I probed, testing him, as I leaned back in my chair and took a sip of wine.

"You have to trust me, Monica. Something doesn't add up, and it all points back to the chief." He was now standing, looking out at the lake. He was upset, I could see; maybe I needed to take his theory to heart. I limped over to join him.

"Guess I don't have many options, for now, but to trust you and your theory. Do you think the chief knows who I am and why I'm here? Did you discuss this with Steven?"

"No, I haven't said a word to Steven. He has enough to deal with, and I don't have any hard evidence to implicate the chief and the department."

I moved in close to him. "Then we need to find that hard evidence, don't we?"

"We do. Where do we start, Monica?"

"To tell you the truth, I've never had to take on a case where the police are involved. If your theory is right, we'll be stepping into some dangerous water."

He smiled, kissing me on the cheek. "Guess we will. You look like your wine medication is wearing off. Why don't you take two of those painkillers I gave you and get some sleep?"

"The doctor is always right." I kissed him gently on the lips, taking his hand, I led him back into the house.

"Am I staying or going?" he asked, grinning.

I wanted him to stay, but I also knew that my mind needed to remain detached and focused on the case, now more than ever. A more significant challenge was forthcoming, more than I would have ever dreamed.

"Doctor, your house call is over. You're going. Tonight, anyway."

Again, I blushed.

Chapter 5

A peaceful night's sleep didn't happen. Wonder why? I now had a partner on the case, one I was already falling for ... Oh, and I had a possibly corrupt police department to deal with. And my cover was likely blown.

After taking a hot shower and drinking three cups of coffee, I walked out onto the deck overlooking Ashbee Lake. I wanted it to talk to me. I wanted the trees to tell me what they saw the night of the murders. I wanted a place to start, which meant the first place would be going over the files on my desk. I sat down at the desk and began to open the police files when my cell rang.

"Good morning." It was Trevor.

"Hello, Dr. Bowen. To what do I owe the pleasure this early in the morning?"

"Er ... just wondered how you're feeling. How's the foot?" I could tell he was making small talk.

"I think a little better, but I'm sure you didn't just call to discuss my foot."

"You're right, I didn't."

"Then, Doctor Bowen, what can I do for you this beautiful morning?"

"I have some time this afternoon. Thought I could pick you up and we can have lunch at Flynn's?"

"I remember that place. I parked in front of it my first day in town when this Prince Charming came up and asked me if I was lost." I was glad he couldn't see the big smile on my face. "That sounds nice, Trevor. But I can drive myself into town? What time?"

"One o'clock okay, Christy?"

I took that as meaning the game was on. *I guess Christy Manning attorney at law it is.*

"See you then."

I was a little surprised that he wanted to be seen with me in public but also interested in some of the local color.

What do you wear to lunch in Ashbee Cove? My choices were limited since Andy made sure I only had "mountain-girl" attire. Jeans, shirt, no makeup, hair in a ponytail; still couldn't wear my boots, which meant flip-flops.

I drove into town and found a parking space right in front of Flynn's. I waited for a few minutes, watching people coming and going, most of the patrons being law enforcement. Interesting. I was just getting out of the Jeep when Trevor appeared out of nowhere.

"You look lovely, Christy. Glad you're not overdressed." He smiled, taking my arm to help me up the curb.

Flynn's was dark, with the smell of whiskey and cigars. It was evident they weren't aware of the California law prohibiting smoking of any kind in a public place. Or they just didn't give a shit.

"Your eyes will adjust." He squeezed my arm. "Follow me. I see a table in the back corner." I followed him, trying not to trip over tables and chairs.

He pulled out my chair. "Thank you, Trevor."

"Well, this is Flynn's—the only place in town with good Irish food."

Was he joking? "Irish food?"

"You'll find out shortly. Just let your eyes adjust a little more."

"You'll have to educate me on Irish cuisine."

Finally, my eyes were adjusting to the dim lights. A quaint place with Irish memorabilia on the walls, an old jukebox sat in the corner, playing some Irish music but not too loudly.

A long bar, with high-back bar stools and in the back, a couple of pool tables and one wall of dartboards.

"This place is about as authentic as you can get. I was in Ireland years ago, and all the pubs looked like this."

"It's very charming. Everyone seems to be enjoying themselves," I said, referring to the laughter of the men playing darts and good old conversation between the patrons sitting at the bar.

"You're about to meet the owner, Johnni Flynn." He nodded in the direction of a beautiful redhead with emerald-green eyes approaching our table.

"Well, if it isn't our favorite coroner. Been a while since you've been in, Trevor. Who's your guest?"

By the way she was standing and her voice, Johnni looked and sounded like one woman you wouldn't want to mess with. She reminded me of Jennie Hodgers.

Trevor stood up. "Johnni, this is Attorney Christy Manning."

"You must be the attorney staying at the Barnes place?"

I smiled. "Yes, I am. Word travels fast here in Ashbee Cove."

"Small town, big mouths. I hear you're also the mermaid the boys almost caught in the lake."

"Ah. Your small town has quite the pipeline."

"Don't worry. There's nothing in this town that happens that I don't hear about first." She flipped open her order pad. "What can I get you two. Lunch or just drinks? Corned beef just came out of the oven, Trevor."

"Then we'll have two of your corned-beef specials, Johnni, and two Kilkenny."

"Excellent choice." She winked at Trevor and walked away.

I noticed that she went over and talked to some men at the bar. I also noticed that the four men, in police-officer uniforms, kept staring at us.

Trevor must have seen them also. "Those are four of the officers that responded to the murder scene."

"Oh. They seem very curious as to who I am." I grinned.

"These guys just haven't seen such a beautiful woman in our town before."

That lightened up my paranoia.

Johnni approached the table with our Kilkenny and sandwiches. "Enjoy." Contrary to how friendly she was initially, she now seemed a little rude.

Taking a sip of the icy beer, I said, "Your redhead's attitude has changed."

"She's just Johnni. The woman is tough, though—don't let those beautiful green eyes deceive you."

The situation reminded me of a story from history about a woman named Jennie Hodgers. She disguised herself as a man and fought side by side with the men during the Civil War. There were four hundred documented such women. The Union Army had Jack Williams, a hard-drinking, tobacco-chewing, foul-mouthed son of a bitch, who was outstanding on horseback, deadly with a sword, and a damn good poker player. Jack fought in eighteen battles, was wounded three times, and taken prisoner once. Yes, Jack was a woman. Which came as quite a surprise when revealed. Her real name was Frances Clayton. Johnni Flynn was like Jennie Hodgers and Frances Clayton all rolled into one small stick of dynamite.

We finished our meal. Trevor went up to the counter to pay the bill. I watched his interaction with Johnni and wondered if they might have had some romantic history. He returned with a scowl on his face.

"What's wrong?"

"Nothing, really," he said. "Johnni might be just a tad jealous of the 'new girl in town.'"

"Do you and Johnni have a romantic past?"

"Hell no. That woman is a ballbreaker and scares me!" he laughed as he helped me up from my chair. "Let's get out of here, I don't like the vibes. And I think she might be involved in the killings. I just don't know how yet. What you see isn't always what you get around here."

Interesting that our visit to town was providing me with new insights.

Once outside, my eyes had to readjust to the bright sunlight. The air was warm and humid. Trevor helped me down the curb and into the Jeep.

"It's a beautiful day. Perfect time to take a dip in the lake. How about we go back to the cabin for a swim?"

"Are you serious? Last time I took a little dip in that lake, I ended up almost losing my foot!" I had to laugh, but he was serious.

"Okay. *I'll* take a swim; you can sit on the deck and tell me the direction of that 'thing' you cut your foot on."

I did want to find out what was on the bottom of the lake. "Okay. I'll meet you at the cabin." Trevor went to get his Hummer from behind his office. I started back to the cabin.

***

A short time later, Trevor showed up. The temperature outside was still warm, and the sun was still high in the sky. I went out on the deck to wait for him. Since I still didn't have a swimming suit, I threw on a pair of shorts and a tank top. If push came to shove, I could easily use the outfit as a swimsuit. I could hear the Hummer's engine approaching the house. Trevor walked down the boat ramp to the dock, where the Crystal Blue was anchored.

He waved. "Aren't you coming in?"

"No, you go ahead! I'll just sit here and sip some wine, if you don't mind."

Trevor dove from the end of the dock into the lake. A few seconds later, he surfaced and swam to the ladder on the deck. I watched as his wet body climbed the ladder, emerging like a god from the depths of the sea. He walked over to me and started shaking his head, throwing water all over me. "I think I found what cut your foot."

"Really? What?"

I handed him a towel to dry off his wet head. "Looks like an old trunk. I think we should get it out of the water."

"And we are doing that how, Doctor Bowen?"

"I have a winch on the Hummer. I'll go down and hook it to the cable, and you can be in the Hummer pulling it up. What do you think?"

Being curious as to what damaged my foot, I said, "Sure, just show me what to do."

"Okay. Meet me at the boat ramp." Trevor went to get the Hummer, and I joined him on the boat ramp.

"All you have to do is get in and put it in reverse. The winch is automatic and will start dragging it from the bottom of the lake. When you see the trunk, just hold steady."

"Got it."

Trevor dove back into the water with the end of the cable, then surfaced, giving me a thumbs-up. I could feel the winch pulling the trunk towards the surface. There it was: an old rusty steamer trunk. Like you might have seen years before on a cruise ship. Finally, the trunk was resting at the top of the ramp. I watched as Trevor kept an eye on our find. He gave the signal to turn off the engine. I got out of the Hummer and joined him by the algae-covered old trunk.

"Now what do you want to do, Monica? It's your trunk." He smiled.

Feeling excited as to what might be inside, I said, "Come on, let's open it."

"Why not? First, how about we drag it up to the back of the cabin?

"Good idea."

"We'll need some bolt cutters to pop this lock. I saw a shed in the back. You go back to the cabin; I'll take care of the trunk." Trevor got into the Hummer and started dragging the large trunk up the driveway and around to the shed. I went back to meet him. He unhooked the cable from the winch, recoiling it and then went to the shed, returning with some large bolt cutters. "This should do the trick."

"Hold on, Trevor. Take a good look at that lock. It looks ancient." I took the lock in my hand. Rusted, with a twisted grapevine pattern, it looked medieval. "Okay, go ahead, but try and keep the lock intact if you can."

Taking care not to destroy the lock, he made one cut, sliding it through the latch on the trunk. "Ready to see what's inside?"

Feeling apprehensive, I said, "Go ahead."

Trevor opened the heavy lid of the trunk. It was dry on the inside. The only thing we could see was a crimson cloth. Gently, Trevor unfolded it.

"What the hell is that?" I asked.

"It looks like a cross."

"Let's take it inside so we can get a better look. Is there anything else in the trunk?" I watched as he felt around the inside.

"No, just this old cross."

Trevor rewrapped the cross in the red cloth, and we both walked inside, excited to get a better look. He placed it on the desk, in the library.

"I don't know about you, but I could use something cold to drink other than lake water."

"You're still wet from that excursion in the lake," I said. "Why don't you take a hot shower? I'll make the drinks. Use the master-bedroom bath; fresh towels are in the cabinet. I won't mess with the cross until you get back." Although I was tempted, he did go to a lot of work getting that trunk out of the water.

"Thanks." He walked to the master bedroom.

I kept thinking about why someone would dump an old trunk with a cross inside into the lake. It looked very old, so it must have had some religious meaning to whoever left it behind. I stepped behind the bar to make some martinis. Then my mind flipped to James Bond's famous line, "shaken, not stirred." I had to smile as to how many times these trivial things popped into my brain at the weirdest moments. I walked back to the desk with our martinis just as Trevor was entering the library after his shower. Of course, I wasn't expecting him to be standing there almost naked with a towel wrapped around his waist.

"How was your shower, and do you plan on just wearing a towel for the rest of the evening? Not that I mind. That little towel looks great on you, Doctor Bowen." I gave him a wink.

"Sorry about that! My clothes are in the Hummer. Don't suppose you've seen any men's clothing sitting around the cabin?"

Funny, he should ask. "I did see a man's robe in the master closet. It probably belonged to Michael."

"Thanks." He left to put on something with a little more coverage. Alas. With that Adonis body of his, I was just fine seeing him half-naked for the rest of the night.

A few minutes later, he came back to the library, wearing a mid-calf chocolate-brown terry-cloth robe. "Is that better? I should have just gone to the Hummer and got my damn clothes." He laughed.

"You look fine. Let's get a better look at the cross in the light." I handed him his drink.

Trevor unwrapped the cross again from the crimson cloth, lifting it towards the light of the lamp, sitting on the desk.

"It's breathtaking! My God, Trevor, what have we found?"

It was a perfectly preserved solid-gold cross, appearing to be of Celtic origin. It was eight inches long, eight inches wide with intricate carvings, which looked like limbs or branches. What took our breath away was what was in the middle of the cross.

"This stone, Trevor ... It's the largest blue sapphire I've ever seen!"

"Are you sure it's a sapphire?"

"Yes. I know my stones, especially expensive ones. Let me get out my laptop and do some research; we're just sitting here staring at something we don't know anything about. Could you go back and get the lock from the trunk? It might give us a timeline to work with."

Trevor left, and I started up the computer. He returned and put the lock on the desk.

"See if you can find a measuring tape around here, maybe look in the kitchen."

After a short search, he found one. I took it and measured the lock first, entering the dimensions into the computer: "56 mm (2.2") wide, 66 mm (2.6") 27 mm (1.06") thick. Iron-carved brass panels."

The research didn't yield much, other than it probably came from China, the Middle East, or the UK. And it was centuries old. I entered the cross next: "304.8 mm (12 x 12") with a 6" circle in the middle encasing a blue sapphire."

There was little I could find on the stone, which led me to believe it was never discovered or registered. Someone simply found it and used it in the making of the cross?

Shrugging my shoulders, I said, "We didn't find much, did we?"

"On the contrary. We found something ancient and priceless. Now, what do we do with it? Hide it?"

I remembered what Steven had included in the original packet he sent me. "I think I have the combination to a safe." I started going through the papers on the desk. "Here it is."

"I recall Michael opening a safe one time when I was here. It's behind the family painting above the fireplace." He walked over to the painting, lifted it carefully, and placed it on the bar.

"Steven sent me some numbers on this piece of paper when he hired me." I started turning the dial, entering the numbers. It opened.

"This looks like as safe a place as any to keep it. Don't you think?"

He handed me the cross, and I placed it inside. Trevor rehung the painting. I stood back looking at the family portrait. Each pair of eyes seemed to stare at us, watching the situation unfold.

"I know this sounds far-fetched, but I wonder if this cross belonged to the Barnes family. It could have been buried in that lake for who knows how long."

He took my glass to refill our martinis as I sat on the barstool, watching him make our drinks. "I remember reading in one of the police reports that blood-splattered navigation maps were found lying on a table in the wheelhouse. He must have been looking at them before he was killed."

"You're right," Trevor agreed. "There were two maps, if I recall. Navionics and depth maps of Ashbee Lake."

"Could this just be a coincidence that this cross was found so close to the Ashbee estate and the Crystal Blue? I mean, could the family have been killed because the killers wanted the cross? Obviously, neither Michael nor Sarah gave up the secret. But we don't know if it had anything to do with the cross, right?"

"You're the professional investigator, but I think we might be onto something."

There's that word "we" again. I hadn't known Trevor long, but my gut was telling me he was one of the good guys, someone who wanted to find out who murdered his friend; and I felt his attachment and concern for the town was genuine.

He stepped from behind the bar, sitting down next to me. "I need to be involved in this. I don't have a choice. Please let me help. I owe this to Michael."

"You can help, Trevor. But I take the lead on this. We've got four people deceased, a possibly corrupt police department—their chief being a prime suspect in the murders—and we have an unhappy redheaded bar owner who might be involved."

He smiled. "Sounds confusing when you say it."

"It's not confusing at all. It's manic and full of what-ifs. Look, it's getting late and the cross is secure. Tomorrow is another day to sort all this out. I'll see you in the morning."

"You don't think I'm leaving you here alone tonight, do you?"

I looked at him with raised brows. "Thanks for the concern, but I'll be okay. Honest."

"It's not that I don't think you can take care of yourself; you can do that better than I can. What if someone saw us salvage the trunk from the lake? Did you pay any attention to our surroundings? I sure didn't."

A good point. I did glance around—natural instinct. But I was hardly thorough. What if someone did see us? Now we were both getting paranoid.

I smiled at him. "You can stay here if it makes you feel more comfortable." His offer to stay made me much more at ease, but I didn't want him to know that.

"Great. Where do you sleep?" A sheepish nod of his head.

"Sorry to disappoint you, Doctor Bowen. You can sleep in the master; I'm already set up in the front bedroom."

"That's a big bed to be sleeping in alone."

"Then if you think it's too big for you. You can sleep on the couch."

He sighed. "No, the master will be just fine, thank you, Miss Wade."

"Trevor, tomorrow I'd like to go aboard the Crystal Blue. I need to see for myself what exactly happened that night."

"Are you sure your foot can handle climbing around the yacht?"

"I'll be fine, but just from the photos I have and the files ... I need to see for myself."

"Then we can do that first thing in the morning."

"I can do it myself. You don't have to come with me. I'm sure you have work to do."

"Nothing that can't wait for a bit. Besides, I need to explain what I think happened. All the evidence being trampled on. It still pisses me off that the chief didn't secure the scene."

"Ok, but remember. I'm the investigator here. This is my case. I don't mind you being involved, and I understand why you need to help. But my case, my call."

"Deal. I won't say another word. You can investigate and I'll just stand by to assist."

"Then we both better get some rest. Sleep well, Mr. Bowen."

There was something about this man that made me want to keep him close. I had an undeniable physical attraction to him. *But do I trust him yet? Not sure.*

Shea Adams

Chapter 6

I woke up to the smell of freshly brewed coffee. I got dressed and walked into the kitchen.

"Good morning, Miss Wade. Coffee?"

He was standing near the stove, flipping what looked like pancakes.

"You're up early, Doctor Bowen."

He handed me a cup of coffee. "Breakfast will be ready in a minute. Hope you like blueberry pancakes. They're my specialty."

Where the hell did he get blueberries? I looked at him with adoration. How could he look this great this early in the day? "What time did you get up?"

"Early." He tossed the pancakes onto a plate.

"Where did you find blueberries? I don't remember buying any."

"Ah, my secret. It's a beautiful morning; take your coffee outside to the deck, and I'll be out in a minute."

Trevor was right. The weather was perfect, and the lake was calm, with a slight briskness in the air. Add the smell of pancakes being made by a man like Trevor. I sighed. *Doesn't get much better than this.*

Trevor soon came out onto the deck with a plate of pancakes, heated syrup, butter, and chopped pecans. "Here you go, Miss Wade. Can I make them up for you?" He wore a nervous smile.

I just couldn't help but share in his excitement over a stack of pancakes. "Mmm, sure ... What a pleasant surprise: the coroner can cook."

He assembled my two pancakes, butter spread evenly over both, placing the pecans on top, then, with painstaking accuracy, slowly poured the warm syrup in a circular motion, making sure there was no dry pancake visible.

"Looks great, Trevor. Thank you." I took the first bite.

"What do you think?"

Taking a napkin, I wiped a bit of syrup off my chin. "Superb."

He smiled, pleased. "So, what's on the agenda for today?"

"The Crystal Blue, remember? Like I said last night. I can do this without you."

"Enjoy your breakfast and we'll go aboard."

***

With breakfast finished and Trevor cleaning up the mess he made in the kitchen, I looked again at the files on the desk, sorting through what little evidence there was. Getting aboard the Crystal Blue, I hoped, would give me more answers to the many questions I had floating around in my mind.

"Ready?"

"Yep. Are you sure you want to go through this again?"

The Ashbee Cove Murders

"I'm sure. To tell you the truth, with all that happened that night when I got the call about the killings, I may have missed something. I've gone over it a thousand times, questioning my findings—or lack of."

Trevor and I boarded the Crystal Blue. Nothing had been touched since the initial investigation took place. I was a bit surprised since the murders happened over six months ago. There was yellow tape still blocking off some sections of the yacht.

"Where do you want to start, Monica?"

"Let's start at the helm where Michael was found."

We climbed the ladder to the helm.

"Michael was sitting here?" I stood behind the captain's chair, looking at the photo of his lifeless almost beheaded body slumped in the chair and down at the now-dried blood pool.

"From what I could tell, his death was instant. A knife was used to cut his jugular and ..." Trevor looked away.

"So, whoever accosted him did it swiftly." I looked at the metal ladder we had just ascended. "I don't see from the remaining blood-splatter stains that he put up much of a fight. They needed him out of the way first because he would have put up one hell of a fight if he knew his family was in danger."

Trevor nodded. "Yes, I agree. And then there was this. There were maps of Ashbee Cove. I surmised that he was looking over them when he was attacked. I found bloodstains. The pictures are in the file I gave you."

"I saw them, but I didn't see the maps themselves ...?"

"I gave them to the chief."

I thought a moment. "Why didn't the killers take the maps, if they were looking for the cross? That doesn't make sense ... Although, at this point, we're only assuming that might have been the motive, though.

"Us finding the cross ... That must have been what they were after. But why not just threaten him and make him tell them where the cross was? They didn't have to kill everyone."

"Trevor, Michael didn't know where the cross was—that's why he was looking at the charts. I'm sure that pissed them off and why they left them behind. Murderers don't think; they just act. You noted there were no fibers or forensic evidence. Not even hair etc.?"

"By the time I got the call and with everyone wandering around the crime scene, it was hard to filter out what might have been left behind from the killers or what those idiot officers left behind. The place was a disaster." Trevor hit his fist on the control panel.

"This isn't your fault. If I was to guess, your theory is correct: whoever did this *wanted* the scene compromised. You okay? Sure you want to continue?"

He nodded. "Yeah. C'mon, the kids were found below." We descended into the cabin where Abby and Stevie were found.

I looked at the photos. Each child was sleeping on their stomach. Overpowering them would have been easy. The shot to the back of the head was execution style. Murderers don't change their killing habits, even for children.

Only, why the fuck would they kill these innocent children? The only answer I had was to ensure no witnesses left behind. Which led me to believe that the killers weren't wearing masks.

I looked around the stateroom, still filled with some of their toys. Stevie was into Star Wars action figures and pirates. Abby had a fondness for horses and unicorns. One stood out. A rainbow-colored unicorn, the name 'Happy' monogrammed on the pink saddle. I sat down on Abby's berth. Picking up the unicorn, I saw something that shouldn't have been there: a feather.

"Trevor, a silencer was used? You didn't mention that in your file, or maybe I didn't catch it?"

"Yes, the killer used a pillow and a silencer. Abby was killed first, then Stevie. They didn't have a chance."

"Again, Trevor, why was this information not included in your reports?" I allowed my tone to show disapproval of the lack of details stated in his findings.

"It was included! It's all in the paperwork and files I sent to Armstrong. Are you accusing me of covering up evidence?"

"No, no, sorry. It's ... I must have skipped over it when I read the files he gave me."

"Right."

The last thing I *wanted* to do was make Trevor defend his actions, but simple pushing, finding buttons often divulges truths. I would go back and read through the files again and check exactly what was and what wasn't in there.

"We should go to the galley where we found Sarah," Trevor said, avoiding eye contact. He turned and led the way.

His silence told me a lot more about what he must have dealt with, investigating a murder scene where evidence was being destroyed. Either on purpose or from shoddy police work.

Nothing had been touched or cleaned up in the galley: dishes broken, chairs turned over, and the faded outline of where her body was when she was found.

"It surprises me no one has cleaned up the yacht. It's been over six months."

"Steven was informed that our investigation was over. I don't know why he hasn't had a professional cleaner come in." Trevor sighed.

"Good thing for us he hasn't." I picked up a broken dish near the galley door. "No fingerprints?"

"None. Why?"

"It's obvious Sarah put up a struggle. She was throwing anything she could get her hands on at the killer or killers." I looked around. *Hello ...* I saw a piece of frayed rope on the ground next to an overturned chair. "She was tied up?"

"Rope burns were found on her wrists."

"I read that she was stabbed a number of times. And raped." I set the overturned chair upright and sat down. "Trevor, sit down, please." When he hesitated, I added, "Please. I need you to relax and talk to me."

I took a breath and positioned myself as if I was Sarah, putting my hands behind my back. "Tell me about the stab wounds. Which one was the fatal one?"

A pause before he rushed out, "The wounds were all over her body. Back, chest, leg, and both arms. The stab to her heart is what killed her. All the others were superficial."

I nodded. "Okay ... then we can speculate that she was being questioned. Maybe about the cross or something important enough to kill for. What I don't understand is the rape. That seems a bit much, don't you think? Considering it happened after she was already dead or bleeding to death in a pool of blood on the floor. It takes a really sick individual to do something like that."

"She was raped with a broom handle. There was no semen found." He paused and massaged his temples. "I did find evidence of wooden fibers and tearing of the vaginal wall. The broom was found, not in the galley but on the dock. There were blood traces on the handle and vaginal fluid, no semen."

I looked at him intensely. "Sarah was killed by a woman, Trevor."

His expression showed his shock. "What? Why would you say that?"

"Superficial wounds indicate to me hesitation from the killer. The broom handle was a symbolic gesture. If she was raped by a man, you would have found much more evidence: pubic hair, semen. The fact the rape was done postmortem, the broom left on the dock. It was the last straw for the killer's frustration. Our killer was a woman, at least in Sarah's case. I'd stake my reputation on it, Trevor."

"Then if my theory is right, Johnni Flynn *is* one of them. I knew it! That bitch!"

"Slow down, Trevor. Let's keep our wits about us here. Where was Flynn that night?"

"When I arrived on the scene, she was leaving to take Paul Kennedy back to town. He's the one who found the bodies.

Out for a walk. He thought he heard Barnes call out to him and boarded when he got no reply. He was very shaken up over finding the bodies. There was so much confusion. I didn't give it a thought. How could I have been so stupid with all of this? I'm a goddamn coroner. It's my job to figure these things out!"

I stood and crossed over to him, placed my hand gently on his shoulder. "That's enough for now, eh? Let's get back to the house. There's one more thing I want to do today. I'm going into town and talk to Flynn."

"Right. I'll co—"

"By myself."

***

Trevor didn't like my idea of talking to Johnni Flynn, but I knew that I needed to get a feel for who she was. I was sure I could ask her some questions about the murders without raising a red flag. Or at least I hoped so.

Trevor went back to his office. I told him after I met with Flynn I would call him. I also wanted to get a better feel for the town. So far, my time had been somewhat chaotic. I drove into town and parked in front of The Quill & Ink bookstore. I loved to browse through old books, especially poetry. I wandered around for a few minutes until a young woman approached, asking if I needed any help.

"Can I help you find something?" Her voice was soft with a slight Irish accent.

"Just browsing." I turned my attention to a display of poetry from such authors as Frost, Maya Angelo, Poe, and Shakespeare.

"Are you interested in poetry, Miss Manning?"

I was somewhat shocked she knew my name, but in this small town it appeared there were no strangers, or if you were one, it was no secret. "You know who I am?"

"Aren't you the attorney for the Barnes family? My friend at the police station told me a beautiful woman came in with a hurt foot to talk to Chief Armstrong." She looked down at my still-wrapped foot wedged into its flip-flop.

"Word does travel fast." I grinned as I picked up a book by Angelo.

"I love her poetry. She's so inspiring. Don't you think?"

"Yes, I do. How long has your bookstore been here?"

"Oh, it's not my store. It belongs to my grandmother, Isabella. She's owned it for almost fifty years. When she and my grandfather migrated here from Ireland, via a brief stop in England, she became inspired by all the lovely bookstores around England. At a very young age, she wrote poetry about their travels to the United States. When they arrived here in Ashbee Cove, my grandfather opened up a furniture store. He handcrafted the furniture himself. Then when the business grew and he no longer needed my grandmother's help, she opened up Quill & Ink." She picked up a book off a nearby shelf. "This is a book of my grandmother's poetry."

I took the book and just from looking at the cover, I knew that the words inside would be something I would enjoy. "Is the book for sale?"

"Oh, yes. It's in its third print. People love her poetry."

"Then I must give it a read."

"Miss Manning ... is Steven Barnes doing ok? We are still devastated by what happened to the family. Abby and Stevie would come in with their mother, Sarah. I would sit with them, and we would read books together while Sarah went shopping. Other parents in town leave their children here while they shop. It's a safe place for the kids who love to read in our kid's nook." She pointed to one corner of the store that was set up with educational toys, tables, and chairs for the kids.

"Steven is doing the best he can, under the circumstances," I assured her.

"Would you like a cup of tea? I blend it myself."

I thought for a moment. The atmosphere was so relaxing, and I might find out more about the town. "That would be nice, thank you."

"Oh, my name is Veronica. Please come and sit. I'll get us some tea." She ushered me to a table in front of the store window with two antique-looking high-back chairs.

"Did your grandfather make these chairs, Veronica?"

"He did. Everyone in town was sad when he passed a few years ago. Since you're staying at the Barnes cabin, you probably have sat on some of his creations. Michael bought a few pieces of my grandfather's furniture. Michel was very proud of a desk chair that my grandfather made specially for him." She poured us a cup of tea.

I took a sip of the aromatic blend. "Mmm, this is delightful. Do you sell it here in the store? I'd love to purchase some. Nothing better than a great book of poetry and a warm cup of tea."

"I do have a few tins for sale. How long will you be staying in Ashbee Cove?"

"I'm not sure. There's still much of the town I'd like to explore. Do you have any suggestions?"

"Ashbee has many beautiful shops. Have you been down to the river area yet? Tourists come here to take pictures and have picnics under the willow trees. It's magical." She smiled.

"I haven't, but I'll put it on my list of places to see."

We chatted a while before I looked up at the old clock on the wall above the entrance door. "This has been so nice, Veronica. I should be going, though."

"I have enjoyed meeting you, Miss Manning. I hope you come back."

"Christy, please. I will."

Veronica smiled and went to the register to ring up my books of poetry. "Consider the tea a gift. I'm so glad you enjoyed it."

I left with a better understanding of how unique the history was in Ashbee Cove. Michael and Sarah had a love for this place and the residents. For their lives to be cut short—and here—was unconscionable. I visited a few more shops: The Wick, a candle shop, as well as The Pied Piper music store and The Rare Spice.

I picked up something for Andy in each shop, knowing how he loved getting gifts from my travels. Now it was time to go visit Johnni Flynn.

I walked into Flynn's place, adjusting my eyes to the dark interior. I heard a voice call out my name.

"Miss Manning! There's an empty seat here at the bar." It was Flynn.

My arms still full of gift bags for Andy, and my eyes finally adjusting, I saw Johnni standing behind the bar.

"Have a seat. Looks like you've got your hands full." Johnni smiled.

"Yes. I finally had a few moments to do some shopping and look around town. It's quite special."

"I thought you'd already gone home. Hadn't seen you around."

"Oh. I was going to leave, then decided to stay a couple more days. Give this damn foot a chance to heal up a little more."

"What can I get you?" Johnni set a cocktail napkin in front of me.

"Something light and refreshing," I said, setting my bags on the floor next to my barstool.

"Gin and tonic with a twist?"

"Sounds great, thanks."

"No Trevor today?"

"I think he's working. Nice to have girl time, alone. If you know what I mean." I smiled.

"I know. Men can be overbearing at times. Guess that's why I'm still single. Don't want anyone telling me what to do." She laughed.

I raised my glass. "Then here's to all us single ladies."

"How much longer are you going to stay in our little town, Miss Manning?"

"Johnni, please call me Christy. I'm done with the paperwork Mr. Barnes needs to settle the estate. In a way, I hate to leave."

"I'm sure you have a busy life to get back to in Malibu."

I had to think quickly. How did Johnni know I was from Malibu? I didn't think Trevor would divulge that information. Maybe I mentioned it to Armstrong without realizing it? However she found out, I needed to keep my cool. "Yes, it'll be nice to finish up here and get home. But I have enjoyed my stay."

"Do you have a stuffy office to go back to?"

"I go into the office a few days a week. The rest of the time I work from home. You know how that LA traffic is. Bumper to bumper every day, so the firm allows us to do most of our work from home unless it's critical we be in the office."

"Ya. I've been there a couple of times. Didn't like it much. The air stinks and people are rude."

"I'm sorry you had a bad experience, Johnni. Guess it depends where in Los Angeles you are." I needed to change the subject and see what information on the killings I could get from Johnni. The fact that she as now my number-one suspect, I would tread easy. "You mentioned at lunch—which was awesome, by the way—that you don't miss much about what goes on here in Ashbee."

"Like I said, small town and when you own the only bar in town, people like to talk and gossip. Why do you ask, Christy? Something you need help with?"

"Not really. More curiosity than anything. I don't understand how the Barnes family could be murdered and the police have no clues as to why and who might have done it."

"It was terrible what happened. I'm hoping whoever did it is long gone. There's some gossip that Michael was involved with some bad people. He was a great guy, don't get me wrong, but sometimes appearances can be deceiving. Don't you think?" Johnni picked up my glass. "Refill?"

"Sure. Any thoughts as to what Michael may have been involved in? Gambling maybe?"

"Could be. Who knows what happens behind closed doors." She set my refill in front of me.

"I have all sorts of scenarios going through my mind, Johnni. Of course, I do have an active imagination. The first thing I thought of was the Mafia or some sort vendetta." I could tell Johnni was getting a little nervous with all my questions. I decided to back off.

"Your guess is as good as mine. A real tragedy. As far as I know, the police did the best they could to find out who did it. I hear there wasn't much evidence left at the scene."

"I guess not. This has been great, but I better get back to the cabin. Packing to do."

"I'm sure Dr. Bowen will be sad to see you leave. You two seemed to have hit it off rather quickly?"

"He seems like a nice enough guy, and I have enjoyed getting to know him, but Malibu is calling me home. I miss the smog." I chuckled to lighten the mood.

"Christy, someone mentioned they saw you and Trevor pull something out of the lake?"

Did she know about the trunk? "Oh? Dr. Bowen thought he'd check out what I cut my foot on. Some old metal piece of junk he pulled out so no one else would hurt themselves."

"Good for him. Never know what's on the bottom of that lake. Tourists can be irresponsible at times. I'm surprised more people haven't been injured with all the junk that's in those waters. Well, Christy if I don't see you again before you leave, have a safe trip home."

"Thanks, Johnni. It's been a pleasure being in your little town and meeting you and Dr. Bowen." I picked up my gift bags and left with little insight other than Trevor and I were being watched. Which also meant she probably knew I wasn't Christy Manning. Johnni Flynn was smart. I knew that by me staying any longer, not only my life but also Trevor's might be in jeopardy. I still couldn't decide if Johnni was capable of such horrific deeds. But like she said, *appearances can be deceiving.*

***

My mind now focused on what had happened the evening before. "I guess we need to find out more about the cross. I'm going to call Andy and see if he might have some suggestions," I told Trevor.

"I thought we decided that no one should know about the cross until we figure it out first."

"First, Andy is my best friend. Secondly, he knows people who might be able to shed some light on what this cross is or represents. We're aware there is nothing on the internet, or at least the websites we found, so my gut says call Andy. My case, my call."

"You need more coffee. Are you always this anxious in the morning?"

"No. I just know that Andy can help. Yes, more coffee would be nice, thank you."

Trevor cleared the plates and went back inside the cabin to refill our coffees. I could tell he was a little miffed at my suggestion. But I also knew it would be the right move to bring Andy into the mix.

"You think this is a good idea?"

"Yes. Or I wouldn't do it. You have to remember that I do this for a living."

"Since I don't know this Andy character, I'm just a little concerned."

"But I do know this character, Trevor. Let me do my job. You don't have to be a part of this."

"No. I'm in one hundred percent. Call Andy, then." His voice was still a little condescending.

Just as I was picking up my cell to call Andy, it made the Andy tone.

"Good morning, my queen. How goes the walk in the woods?"

"Weird! I was just about to call you."

Andy laughed on the other end of the phone. "I knew that."

"You first, Andy. Why did you call?"

"Well, I have some bad news, good news, and bad news. What do you want first?"

"Sounds like I need to know the bad news first."

"As you wish. You remember my friend Tony, who lives up the beach? He died."

"Oh, Andy. I'm so sorry."

"It was a total shock to everyone. Tony was found naked lying on the beach. The police think he was drunk, took a swim, and drowned."

"It does sound like something Tony would do after one of his parties."

"We had his memorial service yesterday in Vegas. There were at least one hundred people that showed up from all over. His sister lives in Vegas and wanted him buried by his mom and dad, who passed away a few years ago. He would have loved the celebration we gave him."

"I'm sure. If that's the bad news, what's the good news?"

His voice was excited. "I was playing blackjack and won seven thousand dollars!"

"Good for you! I suppose you already spent it." Andy didn't need money. He had more than enough being a trust-fund kid. "You said there was more bad news after the good news?"

"I stayed in Vegas an extra night to be with friends so we could remember all the good times with Tony, so I didn't get home until about 4 a.m. this morning."

Now, knowing Andy as well as I do, I knew something in the tone of his voice: a bomb was ready to be dropped. "And …?"

"You better sit down."

"I am sitting down, Andy. What happened?"

"When I got to your place this morning, it looked like a hurricane had come through. All the drawers were pulled out and dumped on the floor, in all the rooms. Your paintings were lifted off the walls. Shit, there was even stuff taken out of the freezer. It reminded me of what you see on TV when the police come and serve you with a search warrant and leave a mess. But what's strange, Monica, nothing seems to be missing. Not even a toothpick, as far as I can tell."

I just sat there for a few seconds, trying to process what he had just told me. "What you're telling me is someone came in, trashed my house, and didn't take anything?"

"Yep. If something were missing, I would know."

At this point, Trevor could tell that my conversation with Andy was not going well. He whispered so as not to interrupt, "Is everything okay?"

I just shook my head. "Did you call the police, Andy?"

"I called as soon as I saw what condition the house was in. They sent out a couple of cops; they just wandered around, taking notes. Said it was probably just some kids being vandals after a night of drinking on the beach. They left about a half-hour ago."

"Vandals, my ass. Call them back and tell them I want some answers. Did they look for prints, footprints ... anything ...? And how the hell did these 'vandals' get in?"

"This one cop said he thought they came in through the glass slider. Did you know you can lift those right off their tracks and you don't even have to break the glass?"

"Damn it." Trevor stood up. "What's going on, Monica?"

"Is that a man's voice I hear? It's early in the morning. Did he spend the night? Did you sleep with him?" Andy was his usual protective self.

"Oh, shut up, Andy! And no, I didn't. I'll explain later. Do what I said and call the police back out, please. There must be some evidence they left behind."

"Yes, my queen. I'll take care of everything and clean up the mess. Don't worry about anything. I got this." His voice was serious.

"Call if you find out anything, alright?"

"Sure."

"Thanks, Andy. I owe you."

"Indeed, you do, my queen. And Cloe is looking forward to collecting."

I smiled. "What would I do without you, Andy?"

"Let's be sure we never have to find out. Bye, queenie."

I hung up and looked up at Trevor, pacing the deck.

"Is everything okay?" he asked.

I looked at him, smiling despite myself. "Well, it appears some assholes broke into my home and trashed the place. Andy said they were looking for something, but nothing was taken."

"Sorry to hear that."

"It's no big deal. Andy's taking care of it."

"You sure have a lot of trust in this Andy."

"Yes, I do."

"Maybe you should go back home?"

Damn! I forgot to tell Andy why I was calling him. "Crap. I need to call Andy back." I reached for my cell phone. Trevor took my hand.

"Why don't you go back home and take care of that business first. You'll be thinking about it all the time until you physically see everything's okay."

"It's not as if I live around the corner, Trevor."

"You never told me where you live."

Again my thoughts were dragged back to Johnni. She knew I lived in Malibu and Trevor didn't. Christy Manning's cover was blown ... damn it!

"Malibu." I looked at him and smiled.

"Why doesn't that surprise me? Let's get packed."

"Hold on, cowboy. Here's that 'we' again."

"Look, Monica. I have all this time on my hands. My assistant can handle any issues in the coroner's office. I want to go with you. What's wrong with having a little company?"

"Nothing; this isn't your concern is all. I'll just drive back to Malibu, check things out, and be back in a couple of days. I still have a murder case to solve."

The timing couldn't be worse. I needed to stay and see this case through to the end, yet I knew that figuring out why my house had been vandalized with nothing taken was something I needed to attend to. Andy was great, but those little hairs on the back of my neck were telling me there was more to this than punks on the beach getting drunk and picking my house out of a steady line of bungalows along that stretch of beach. Made no sense.

Trevor interrupted my train of thought. "So, am I going with you or staying here?"

No, he needed to stay. Only, I *wanted* him to come with me. Why? "Sure, the company on the road would be nice."

"Great. What do I need to bring along?"

"We're only staying a couple of days. Casual all the way."

"I'll go back to my place, grab a few things, come back, and pick you up." He started for the door.

"No, Trevor. I'll be driving us in the Jeep."

"But I think I can find my way to the Los Angeles basin." His cell phone rang. It was Cari, his assistant coroner. He listened intently, then hung up the phone. "Guess you'll be going back to Malibu by yourself. Cari got a call. Paul Kennedy is dead."

"Oh, my God! You mean the guy who found the bodies on the Crystal Blue?"

"Yes, that Kennedy. I need to go back to the office. I'm sorry."

"No, please. I'll be fine."

He opened the front door, then turned back and walked towards me. He took my face, leaned in, and kissed me. "Call me when you get to Malibu." I watched him walk down the steps.

Stunned at what just happened, I called out to him. "Trevor! Malibu can wait!" The news of Paul Kennedy's death was shocking. Was he murdered?

He rushed back up the steps, grabbed me once again, and kissed me. "I'll give you a call when I find out what happened. I'll keep you apprised of everything. Okay?"

"Okay." I watched until the Hummer was out of sight.

My mind started trying to put thoughts together, but they weren't making any sense. The Barnes family murdered. Trevor and I finding the cross. The break-in at my beach house. Now Paul Kennedy's death. I've been in this business long enough to know things like this aren't coincidences.

I went to the safe, took out the cross, and went over to the couch, unwrapping it from the crimson cloth. I held it tightly as if wanting it to talk.

"Could you be the cause of all this mayhem? Are you ... cursed?"

Of course, it wasn't, but whoever sunk that old trunk in the lake, with the cross inside, never wanted it to be discovered.

Chapter 7

I heard a car come up the driveway, but it wasn't the Hummer. Who could be coming here if it wasn't Trevor? I went to the window and looked out the blinds. It was Chief Armstrong.

What the hell does he want?

I reached for my gun sitting on the entry table and held it behind my back. He knocked on the door.

"Chief Armstrong." *Damn, I forgot to put the cross back in the safe!* It was sitting in plain sight on the coffee table, though it was wrapped in the crimson cloth. Hopefully, he wouldn't notice it.

"May I come in, Miss Manning?" I opened the door, and he stepped inside.

"What can I do for you, Chief?" I tucked my gun inside the waistband of my sweats, covering it with my sweatshirt.

"Just doing my rounds. I like to check on the vacationers camped down by the lake and thought I'd stop by to check on you."

"Thank you, but everything's fine."

"To tell you the truth, I thought you'd already left. I'm surprised to see you still here."

"Yes, Chief. I'm leaving tomorrow. I think I have enough information, thanks to you and Doctor Bowen."

"According to Johnni Flynn, you and our coroner have become good friends." He smiled.

"Strictly business, Chief. My life is way too busy for personal relationships." *What's he after? Does he know my identity?*

"That's a shame. A beautiful woman like yourself should have a man in her life. Trevor's a nice fellow. Did he happen to mention that Paul Kennedy was found dead today?" How did he know Trevor had been here?

I started to lie to him, but I could tell he was waiting for me to slip up. "Trevor was here earlier and got the call that Mr. Kennedy was deceased. He's at the office, I assume."

"Well, I won't keep you any longer, Miss Manning. It's been nice having you visit our tiny town. You have a safe trip home. Please give Steven Barnes my regards."

I opened the door. "Yes, Chief, I will. Thank you again for all your help. I think the family can now move on from this tragedy."

I quickly shut the door. *That SOB knows who I am.* I needed to call Trevor. I waited until the chief's car was down the road.

Taking a deep breath, I called Trevor's number but disconnected the call. *Wait ...* Why should I be in such a panic? Even if the chief did know my real identity, there was nothing he could do about it. If I were found dead along with Paul Kennedy's death, someone would start asking questions. Number one on the list would be Trevor. I wondered how many people he would have to get rid of to cover up the Barnes murders. So far, I counted five. Would he do that? Yes, I believed he would.

I went and sat down on the couch, once again looking at the cross. Now I knew more than ever that this was the key to solving this whole case. My cell phone rang. It was Trevor.

"Hi, Trevor. How you, doing?"

"Not so good, I'm afraid. I haven't finished the autopsy yet, but it's clear Kennedy was murdered. He was found with his throat slit and shot in the back of the head, identical to Michael's wounds.

"Same MO," I noted.

"I can't explain any more over the phone, but get everything together regarding the case—all the files, the cross—and be ready to leave. Okay? I'll be there in thirty minutes." His voice was panicked.

"Okay." Guess I didn't tell the chief a lie. I am going back to Malibu.

Strangely, I always do better under pressure. Pressure has a habit of crystallizing my thoughts and actions. I calmly packed up the files and the cross. My bags were ready. Now I tried to relax in the dead silence as I waited for Trevor.

The Hummer was soon pulling up the driveway. I went outside to the front porch.

Trevor jumped out of the Hummer. "Are you ready to go?"

"Yes, but wait a second and calm down."

We went inside. Trevor took my arm and pulled me close. "Monica, this whole situation is getting ugly. I need you to leave and not look back."

I pushed away from him. "Chief Armstrong was just here."

"What?" Now he was pacing the floor.

"Relax. I told Armstrong I had all the information needed and that I was leaving."

"Good."

"You need to come with me, Trevor. What if you're next? He's apparently cleaning house."

"He wouldn't mess with me. Too many questions he'd have to answer."

"Maybe so, but I think you need to come with me back to Malibu."

He was thinking. "There isn't much more I can do here. Paul's autopsy is basically finished. I can throw his murder back on the chief's desk. He'll have to investigate, which will keep him busy trying to explain to the town why there's been another murder."

"Then I think we should leave together."

"You can follow me back to the office. It'll only take me a few minutes to close everything out. Cari can handle the rest."

We spent the next few minutes closing the cabin and loading the Jeep. Trevor assisted getting me in the Jeep, leaning in to give me one last kiss.

"I'll meet you at the office, Trevor. Please hurry."

I followed him along the windy road towards town. I was thinking that—

From out of a side road, a black SUV came straight at me. I swerved to avoid it, but the SUV hit the Jeep's rear bumper, left corner, sending me into a spin.

What the fuck? I came to rest against a tree that kept the Jeep and me from catapulting over the cliff. I watched the SUV come to a screeching halt. I couldn't see who was driving because of the blacked-out windows. Trevor was driving ahead of me and must have seen what was happening in his rearview mirror; he was already turning around and speeding towards the SUV. The SUV backed up, gunned the engine, and headed straight for me.

As I teetered on the edge of the small cliff, I grabbed my gun, jumped out of the driver's seat, and dove for cover. I fired—three shots—and must have hit the SUV because it stopped, turned around, and started heading towards the Hummer.

Gunshots ... Crap, they were shooting at Trevor! He skidded to a halt in a cloud of dust. They passed me at a high rate of speed as the man in the passenger seat leaned out the window and fired at me. I shrunk back behind a rock. The bullet *pinged!* and I broke into a run towards the SUV and Hummer, heard two more shots fired before the SUV sped away towards town.

Christ no! Please no!

I reached the Hummer. Trevor was slumped over the steering wheel. Blood oozed from his left shoulder.

Shit! "Trevor! Can you hear me? Can you move ...?"

He moaned, and I grabbed his arm and placed it over the shoulder wound. "Press here, Trevor."

He gasped.

"Well done, Doctor. Okay, I need to drive you to the hospital, so I have to get you out of this seat, okay?"

Together, we eased down from the Hummer. "Keep pressing, Doc." I assisted him to the passenger side before I jumped into the driver's seat.

He was barely able to speak. "Monica ... take me back ... cabin. Get files 'n' cross ... I'll be okay."

"Shit, Trevor, are you sure?"

He was beginning to catch his breath now. "Yeah ... They just caught ... top o' the shoulder."

I acquiesced. The Jeep was still on the edge of the cliff, but I retrieved everything, throwing it into the Hummer. Once at the cabin, I helped Trevor inside, sitting him at the kitchen table.

"What do I need to do?"

"Towels. Get me some towels and rubbing alcohol." He groaned in pain.

I got the towels but couldn't find any rubbing alcohol, so I headed for the library to get a bottle of whiskey. When I returned to the kitchen, Trevor had already removed his shirt. Blood was forming a stream of red from the wound.

"Trevor, it looks bad. You need to get to the hospital."

He looked at the bottle of whiskey and smiled. "Pour us both a shot of that and the rest onto the wound. It's not as bad as it looks, the bullet went straight through. Tear the towels and start applying pressure." He took the shot of whiskey. The bleeding was slowing, and I bandaged his shoulder as best I could, with him grimacing as he gave me instructions.

I poured us both another shot of whiskey and helped Trevor to the couch in the living room. "Trevor, someone just tried to kill us."

His head was resting on the back of the couch. "No, Monica. Someone tried to kill *you*. I just got in the way trying to come to your rescue."

"Were they trying to kill me or were they just trying to scare the shit out of me?"

"No, they were trying to kill you, I think. When I looked in the rear mirror, that SUV was headed straight for you. They were going to push you over the cliff."

I nodded. "Maybe." Sitting beside him, I put my head on his bandaged shoulder. "Thanks for coming to my rescue."

"No problem, but would you mind leaning on the other shoulder, please?" He smiled in pain.

"Oh, sorry."

I was just getting up to change my position when I heard a knock at the door. I looked out the window. It was the old man, Charlie Towne. I went to the door and opened it.

"Hi, Mr. Towne. What can I do for you?"

I must have looked a mess because he just stood staring at the blood on my shirt. "Are you okay, Miss Manning?"

"Oh, I'm fine. Just er, cut, myself."

"That must have been an unfortunate accident you were involved in. I was on my way back from town and saw your Jeep on the side of the road. Thought you might need some help."

"Thank you, Mr. Towne, but I can just get it towed."

"Is it drivable? Only asking because Old Sam is the only towing service we got and he's a crook. I can give you a ride up there."

"Well, thank you, Mr. Towne, I mean Charlie. I'll get my keys." I politely shut the door.

"Charlie Towne is going to give me a ride back to the Jeep. I should be able to drive it back here."

"Okay. But be careful, those assholes might come back."

"Maybe. But probably not—not for a while, anyway. I think you spooked them with your timely intervention, Doctor. They'll be planning their next move."

Trevor nodded as he rearranged his position. "As will we when you get back, Miss Wade?"

I nodded. "As will we."

***

I joined Charlie outside and jumped into the front seat of his white Chevy truck. I adjusted my position because of my gun. Charlie, being in the military, noticed it under my shirt right away. "You and that gun are pretty good friends, I see."

A sheepish smile. "Oh, yes. Constant companions. Where I go, it goes."

"I like to see a woman that can take care of herself. My late wife was like you. She packed everywhere. God rest her soul."

The Jeep was still on the edge of the cliff.

"Don't worry, Missy; I brought a towrope. I can pull you away from the edge."

Charlie got his rope from the bed of his truck and wrapped it around the tow hitch of the Jeep.

"Okay, start her up! I'll give you a pull."

It was surprising that the Jeep didn't have more damage. The engine started right up, while Charlie carefully pulled me to a safe spot in the road. He unhooked the rope.

"Looks like you can make it back to the cabin with no problems."

"Thanks so much, Charlie." I waved as he drove away in his truck.

Once back at the cabin, I looked at the Jeep's bumper. Just a few dents ... a few bullet holes. *Great. How am I going to explain this to Andy?*

I walked inside to check on Trevor, who was resting comfortably.

"Everything is fine with the Jeep. Charlie did an excellent job."

"He's one of the good guys."

I noted the pained look on his face. "Trevor, are you sure you shouldn't go to the hospital and just get checked out?"

He motioned for me to sit next to him on the couch. "You know the law in California. The attending physician must report all gunshot victims to the authorities. Which in this case is me."

I nodded. Trevor was right. That would alert the cops. And if they really were part of all this ... Not something we need to deal with right now.

"Okay, Doctor, no hospital. For now. What else can we do?"

"I'll take a couple of those painkillers I gave you for your foot, Miss Wade."

"Sure, I'll go get the bottle. I only took one."

I came back with the pills and a glass of water. "Trevor, you need to rest."

"These will help, thanks. But we need to leave in a couple of hours. The longer we stay in Ashbee Cove, the more danger you are in."

"Just rest." I laid him down on the couch, covering him with a soft Afghan. Sitting on the floor beside the sofa, I took his hand. "You'll be okay ... won't you?"

"Yeah, I'll be fine."

I sat there, looking at his handsome face, admiring the qualities he had. A few minutes later, he fell asleep. His compassion, caring, sense of humor. All the things I wanted in a life partner. Why did it have to happen now?

Am I falling in love with Doctor Trevor? Did butterflies in the stomach count? Or that aching in your heart you read about? *Damn, I think so.*

I decided it was time to call Andy. He needed a heads-up that we were coming back to Malibu.

"Hi, Andy."

"Hey there, my queen. Are you okay?"

"I'm fine, but something has come up, and I'm heading back to Malibu."

"You don't sound a bit fine. What's going on, Monica?"

"Nothing I can talk about over the phone. We'll be leaving in a few hours, putting us home late tonight."

"*We*, like in, you're bringing someone else with you? Who?"

"It's the coroner here in Ashbee Cove. No more questions, Andy. Please. Could you just be at the house when we get there?"

"You sound serious. I know something is wrong. Yes, I'll be here."

I knew Andy didn't like me beating around the bush when he instinctively knew something was up, but I didn't want to elaborate here and now. "Thanks. See you in a few hours." I hung up the phone and went back into the kitchen to clean up the blood from Trevor's wound.

I was also able to get a little rest. Two hours passed. I hated to wake Trevor, but we needed to get on the road. I gently touched his forehead.

"Trevor, we need to leave."

He slowly opened his eyes. "How long was I out?" He sat up, holding his wounded shoulder.

"A couple of hours. We need to leave as soon as possible. Can you travel?"

"I'll be okay. What time is it?"

I checked my cell phone for the time. "Three o'clock. If we leave now, we can be in Malibu in a few hours. The Jeep's running fine. I've already loaded our bags."

"And the cross, the files?"

"In my leather bag and safe."

"Okay, let's go. Give me five minutes to throw some water on my face. Did you get the first-aid bag? Just in case this opens up." He held his shoulder again.

"Trevor, one last time: Are you sure that we don't need someone at the hospital to look at that gunshot?"

"I can take care of it. How are *you* feeling?"

"Besides a bump on my head and a few bruises, Doc, I'm good."

I helped him stand up. From the lack of groaning, he seemed to be okay.

I just hoped he'd stay that way.

Chapter 8

A few minutes later, we were in the Jeep and driving up the same windy road where we had been attacked. I could see the skid marks on the road and the dented tree that had stopped the Jeep from rolling over the cliff.

"Trevor, this is just insane. We almost died here."

"But we didn't." He reached over and patted me on the leg.

I had just started down Main Street when I saw the black SUV parked in front of the police station. "My God, Trevor! Look, it's the SUV."

"Guess my assumption is right. The chief is part of this conspiracy."

I was keeping a close eye on my rearview mirror, making sure that the SUV stayed put and was not following us. We passed Flynn's. Johnni was standing outside. She waved us down, but I just kept driving.

"Wonder what Johnni wants?" Trevor said.

"I assume she was going to try and stall us from leaving town. If she's part of this."

"Yeah, she's part of this. In fact, she might be the leader of the Irish mob, for all I know."

"You think the killings are mob-related? Why?"

"You're the PI, Miss Wade. Who kills people execution style other than the mob?"

I sighed. "Yeah, I have to admit it has all the signs. Or it's an elaborate ploy to make it *look* like a mob hit."

We had been driving for less than an hour when I looked at the gas gauge. "Shit, we need to stop for gas. I know a place right up the road. I stopped there on my way in."

"Are you talking about REDS?" He began to laugh.

"How did you know?" I asked, smiling.

"REDS is famous in this area. Fascinating history."

I turned off the main road, onto the unpaved road towards REDS. "Yes, I was told the legend by the son, or at least that's who I think he was. Kind of an odd fellow with missing front teeth and makes up his own gas prices?"

"It depends on the day, month, or year you stop. I'm surprised he even charged a beauty like yourself. He fancies himself a lady's man."

"You've got to be joking."

I pulled up to the pump. Trevor started to get out of the Jeep to fill the tank.

"You stay put, Doctor. I'll take care of this."

"Sure, you don't need backup?" He laughed through the pain in his shoulder.

Minutes later, I was back.

"How'd it go?"

"Same price as the first time ... pretty much." I drove back onto the main road, and for the next hour, I drove while Trevor slept. It was good to have some quiet time to figure out what to do next with all this new mob information. Andy was right from the first day he heard me talk about the case. I could hear his sweet voice running through my head. "Sounds like a professional mob hit to me, my queen."

Trevor started stirring in his seat. "Sorry about falling asleep. Where are we?"

"Just got onto Highway 1."

"Isn't it a bit odd that the only things I know about you are that you're a PI, you're hot, and you carry a gun?"

I gave him a shy grin. "Guess that's all you need to know."

We drove another few miles through the town of Malibu, heading north along the Pacific. The evening was warm, the Pacific calm, and Trevor was enjoying the scenery. I flicked my signal to make a left turn into the Colony, stopping at the security gate. Harold, the security guard, raised the bar and waved me through.

"Monica, you didn't tell me you lived at the beach."

"You didn't ask."

It was now close to eight o'clock. Because of the time change, the sun was just about to set its glow onto the blue Pacific. I pulled into the driveway and honked the horn. The garage door opened. Andy was standing next to Candy, with his hands on his hips.

"That must be your friend, Andy?"

"Relax, he doesn't bite." I opened the door and got out of the Jeep.

Andy came running up to give me a hug. Then he noticed the bullet holes and the dent in his Jeep's bumper.

"Good to see you, my queen. But *what the hell happened to my Jeep?*"

"Long story, sweetie. I'm sorry, but I will get it fixed. I pointed to Trevor sitting in the passenger seat. "Andy, this is Trevor. Trevor, this is Andy."

"Nice to meet you," they greeted each other in unison.

"Andy, would you mind helping with our bags? Trevor has an injured shoulder."

He looked at me in a way a father looks at the boyfriend you just brought home for the first time. "Sure," he simply said.

I walked around the Jeep to help Trevor.

"I'm not broken, Monica."

I let him do it himself, then assisted Andy with the bags. We walked inside.

Turning to Andy, I asked, "Sweetie, could you put those two bags in the guest room?"

Andy took Trevor's bags. I kept the leather bag with the cross inside with me.

Trevor wasn't saying much, so I suggested he go outside to the deck. "It's a beautiful view this time of evening. Can I get you something?"

"Sure. Scotch if you have it." He walked out onto the deck, sitting at the table.

"I'll be right out. Just relax."

Andy came into the kitchen as I was mixing our drinks. "What *the fuck* is going on, Monica? You look like shit! And is that a gunshot wound in Trevor's shoulder?"

I tried to change the subject. "Looks like the house cleaned up nicely. Wouldn't even know that someone trashed it.

Thank you, you're amazing! Have you noticed anything missing yet, and did you call the police back?"

"Nice try changing the subject. You better be ready to tell me everything, my queen." He gave me a hug. "Are you two hungry?"

Oh, Andy. Always so kind. I could almost cry. "Thanks, that would be great. It's been ... a long day."

I took our drinks and joined Trevor outside. "Andy is making us something to eat." I sat down, taking a deep breath and a sip of my drink.

"Andy seems like a nice guy."

"You have to trust me. Andy will do anything I need him to do."

Andy soon came out with a tray of his bruschetta, some hummus, and fruit. "Hope this is okay, you guys. I didn't know my queen here was coming home so soon. And with a guest."

We enjoyed our food with small talk, which was driving Andy crazy.

"Okay, you two!" he suddenly blurted. "What the hell is going on?"

I looked at Trevor, and he nodded his head. I went into the house and came out with my leather bag, setting it on the table. I opened it and took out the red cloth, gently unfolding it. The sun was just setting; the red sky illuminated the cross.

"Whoa, Lone Ranger. What the fuck is that? Excuse my French, Trevor."

"It's a long story. Not sure where to start."

"From the beginning would be nice. You come home with bruises, and your Trevor has been shot. And my poor Jeep looking like it was in the Saint Valentine's Day Massacre. Start talking."

I began the story of what had been happening in Ashbee Cove. From me cutting my foot to meeting Trevor, pulling the old trunk out of Lake Ashbee, finding the cross, getting shot at from a black SUV, and our conspiracy theory that the chief of police, some of his officers, and a tavern owner were, we suspected, responsible for the Barnes murders. And the killing of one of the witnesses.

Andy was listening, the whole time shaking his head. He spoke. "Well then, let me just sum all of this up. You two have gotten yourselves into a bucket of shit with no shovel."

Trevor had to laugh at Andy, who was trying to be serious. "Yep, that's about right, Andy."

"This is not a joke. Remember what I told you when you first got this case, Monica? Now you two almost get killed, and you're dealing with crooked cops! Jeez, could this movie get any better? Are you sure you didn't steal this thing?"

"It's not stolen. Or we don't think it is, but we have no information on it."

"Can I touch it?"

I handed it to him.

"Crap, it's heavy, so must be solid gold. And that blue sapphire. I think you found the 'holy grail.'"

"We found something, for sure, Andy. What it is we have no idea," Trevor said.

"No shit, Sherlock! Of course, people would kill for this. It's got to be priceless ... Do you think the break-in here was someone looking for this cross?"

"We don't know," I admitted. "It's possible someone saw us pull the trunk from the lake and Chief Armstrong and the bar owner thought I'd already left town. Maybe they thought I had taken the cross with me. They would have had plenty of time to drive here and trash the house looking for the cross. Then when they realized it wasn't here, they went back to Ashbee Cove. When I was run off the road, they obviously thought I had it with me."

Andy smiled. "Well, you did almost get killed. In my unprofessional opinion, they knew you had it, whoever they are. Glad I was in Vegas, or you would have found me dead."

I must say that, telling this story aloud to Andy, it did sound more like a movie script than real life.

"Regardless of the timing, Monica, we need to find out more information on the cross," Trevor said. "Andy, Monica tells me you might know someone who can help?"

Andy was thinking. "Wait a minute. I do know someone. Monica, do you remember the guy that I was seeing. He was the professor of antiquities at the university?"

"The Irishman?"

"Yes, that was my pet name for him. He retired a few years back due to poor health. But he's still alive and living here in the Colony."

"Why would you think he might know something?" Trevor asked.

"Good God, man! Duh! Scotty's like a professor of *old stuff*. I used to sit for hours listening to his stories about some of his archaeological finds. When he was younger, he spent years digging up ancient relics in Ireland, but mostly the Grange area. That's why I call him the Irishman."

Trevor leaned back, holding his shoulder. "Andy, are you perhaps talking about Scott Kavanaugh? He's a legend in the areas of Irish and Egyptian antiquities. I had the pleasure of hearing one of his lectures when I was attending Stanford. Specifically, the Newgrange Passage Tomb. The man is very knowledgeable. Monica, I would trust this man to look at the cross."

I looked at Andy. "Could you give him a call and set up a time for us to meet?"

"I'll call him first thing in the morning—he goes to bed early. I'll make him one of my apple pies. He just loves my pie. Refills anyone?" Andy went for more drinks.

"What do you think, Doc?"

"About, Miss Wade?"

"Andy helping us."

"I think Andy's a good man. I'm impressed that he knows Scott Kavanaugh personally. In more ways than one, I assume. And I think Andy would throw himself in front of a train to save, help, or please you."

"Are you being sarcastic?" I just felt the tone in his voice could be a little less judgmental.

Andy came back with our drinks.

"If you two will excuse me, I'm going to put the cross in the safe."

"Good idea," Andy said. I knew he was anxious to drill Trevor, though not literally, I hoped.

I made my way inside, but I could hear their conversation.

"Sounds like you and Monica have been through a lot in a very brief period of time?"

"She's an amazing woman, Andy."

"Oh, sweetie, tell me something I don't know. She is totally a woman of strength, but with a dash of humanity thrown in. I'm fortunate to have her as my best friend."

"Sounds as if the feeling is mutual. Monica speaks very highly of you and your friendship."

"Man to man, Trevor. Have you slept with her yet?"

"Is that a question you should be asking?"

"Yes, it is. Because if you have and are just playing with Monica's feelings. I will have to kill you."

"Relax, Andy. She's been a perfect lady. Not that I haven't wanted something

more to happen between us, but she made it very clear that she doesn't mix cases with pleasure. So, no, we haven't had sex. And you have my word that I won't hurt her in any way."

The boys stopped talking when I came back out. "Why are my ears burning?"

They both laughed.

"Because we were talking about you?" Andy said. "Why don't you two take a walk on the beach. I'll clean up. Then I need to get home to Cloe, and I know you both are anxious to get some rest."

"Thanks, Andy. We'll see you in the morning."

He waved as he left, and Trevor and I took off our shoes and walked the few steps from the deck onto the cold sand.

"I'm surprised you haven't spent much time in this area, considering you were just up the coast in San Francisco," I said.

Trevor reached over to hold my hand. I didn't resist. We continued to stroll along the beach, allowing the water to recede beneath our feet, knocking us off balance.

"Doesn't this remind you of when you were a kid coming to the beach for the first time?" I asked. "The vast waters that stretched forever and you couldn't see land. When I was little, my father told us the story of Columbus and how people of that era thought the earth was flat, so when you sailed into the horizon you had to be careful or you would fall off the edge of the Earth. Of course, we believed him." I squeezed his hand.

Trevor stopped. Turned me to him and kissed me, and I returned his advance. I felt my body go limp, the aroused feelings pulsing through my veins.

"Monica ... I think I'm falling in love with you."

I smiled before adding, "Trevor, I ... your timing ..."

"Yeah, I know. But what can I say? I feel what I feel."

I gazed into his gorgeous eyes. "I'm not saying I don't feel the same, but do you understand what we might have gotten ourselves into?"

"Yeah. I apologize for making you uncomfortable, and I know your boundaries. Case first. Right?"

"Don't apologize. Let's just hope that at the end of this case, we're both still alive to take this relationship to the next level." I kissed him on the cheek. "We should be getting back. Big day tomorrow, meeting with Kavanaugh."

"I'm looking forward to seeing him again. The man's an icon."

Walking hand in hand, we spent the time just enjoying our surroundings. Trevor was comfortable, reassuring, and stable. Tomorrow, we would hopefully get the information we needed, a better understanding of the cross, and if it could be the reason for these murders. Andy was gone when we got back, and the place was locked up tight. I reached under a small pot near the slider, lifted a piece of the deck board, and pulled out a small tin box with the house key inside.

"That's cute, Miss Wade. Thieves would think to look under the pot for a key, but never the deck itself." I smiled, unlocked the slider, and we went inside.

"I think you'll be comfortable in the guest room, Trevor. You have a private bath; everything you need should be in there."

We were both now standing in the hallway. It felt a little awkward since the man just professed his love for me. But a necessary awkwardness.

"Goodnight, Doctor." I kissed him gently on the lips.

"Goodnight, Miss Wade. You, er, do have cold running water in the shower, right?" He smiled, and I smiled back with a little shake of my head.

Shea Adams

Chapter 9

I woke from a dead sleep, startled. I heard footsteps on the deck and now light scratching on the glass slider. This wasn't unusual since all the beach houses are built on pillars, allowing any rogue waves to go under the house and not through it. Raccoons love their little nests underneath and, occasionally, they would wander up to ravage through garbage cans or from just curiosity of what's going on with the people that live upstairs from them. I refer to them as my "peeping-tom raccoons." I knew it wasn't Andy because he would always announce himself. With recent events, I couldn't be too careful. I pulled my gun from the nightstand drawer and started down the hallway. Trevor must have heard the same noise because I saw him standing in the doorway.

"What's going on?" he said in a whisper.

"I don't know. Just stay behind me."

We crept down the hallway and were just about to turn the corner into the kitchen when I saw two shadows on the deck. "Damn it!" I hissed. "Someone's trying to break in."

I could see their silhouettes in the moon's dim light reflecting off the shimmering ocean surface. One of them had already cut the glass with a cutter and was reaching in to flip the slider latch. Damn.

"They're coming in through the slider. On the count of three, hit that light switch on your left."

Trevor looked across to the switch, then back at me. He nodded.

It's always better to let an intruder enter your premises first before killing them. It makes them an easier target and it saves on paperwork. I counted with my fingers. When my third finger flicked up, Trevor flipped the switch. The only thing these two masked assholes saw was me standing there with a .45 pointed in their direction. Then one of them reached for something in his back waistband. I could tell it was a silver handgun from the reflection in the glass.

"Drop it, ass-wipe!" The other man was already trying to get back out the glass slider, onto the deck. I fired a shot in his direction. I didn't want to hit him, just scare him. The bullet just missed his shoulder, he turned, pointing his gun directly at me and fired. The bullet missed my head by inches and embedded itself in the wall. The second intruder then made his move.

I was faster and shot him in the leg. He dropped to the ground, screaming in pain. His friend, still standing by the slider, pointed his gun and fired off four more shots. Trevor and I took cover. The masked intruder ran from the deck around towards the garage. I took chase but lost him in the darkness.

I went back into the house where Trevor was still standing in shock, just looking at the masked gunman. He was now breathing raspy, ragged breaths. I looked at his chest to see a scarlet stain spread across his top like an ink stain. He'd caught a bullet from his friend. Accidentally or deliberately? I wondered. Shit, he still had the gun in his hand.

"Trevor, damn it! Get his gun!"

The man looked up at me and uttered a haunting, rasping "*Bitch*!" before his eyes glassed over and his breathing ceased.

Even I just stood there a little shocked.

"W-what the hell just happened?" Trevor said, clearly shaken too.

"As best I can tell, two masked guys broke into my house, tried to kill us, and one ended up dead, and the other one escaped."

I walked over to the dead man and pulled off his mask to expose his face. Trevor gasped.

"What? Does this guy look familiar? Maybe one of Armstrong's dirty cops?"

"No ... I-I don't think so."

His reaction was a little surprising, I thought, considering he cut up people for a living.

Taking my phone, I called 911.

"Are you calling the police?" Trevor was clearly very nervous.

"Yes, Trevor. It's customary when there is a dead person in someone's house."

"That means we'll have to answer questions?"

"Okay, Trevor. What's wrong? We have to notify the police; I can't just let this guy rot in my living room. Besides, there is still a gunman on the loose."

"It means we'll have to tell them about the cross. Because that's the only reason two thugs would be breaking into your house. Chief Armstrong sent them."

"I get that. Don't worry. I can deal with it."

"911. What is your emergency?"

"This is Monica Wade at 211 Chambers Way in Malibu Colony. There were two armed gunmen in my house. One of them is dead. The other one escaped."

"Okay, understood. Ma'am, did you defend yourself with a firearm?"

"Yes. I'm a licensed PI."

"Are you still armed?"

"Yes, I'm still holding my gun."

"Are you hurt?"

"No."

"Okay, the police and ambulance are on their way. Please stay on the line with me until they arrive."

"Okay." She was probably wondering why I was talking so calmly on the phone—what with a dead body in my house.

Trevor was still standing over the man. "Trevor, please go sit down. The police are on their way. I'll handle this. Just relax."

We both heard the siren as the ambulance came down Chambers Way. My beach house is at the end of the narrow street. Shortly after, we heard the police sirens right behind them.

"Trevor, I'm going outside to the front. The ambulance and police are here. I need to release my weapon to them. Are you okay for a few minutes?"

"I'm all right."

He's still shaken. I smiled, then walked to the front of the house, holding my hands in the air, with my weapon in plain sight.

"Monica Wade? Turn around and place your weapon on the ground. Back up slowly to the sound of my voice." I recognized the voice. It was Derrick Edwards. I did as he requested.

"Okay, Monica. Put your hands down." I turned around to face Derrick.

I grinned sheepishly. "Well, hi, Derrick."

"What the hell is going on here? The dispatch said there's a dead man and a woman with a gun?"

"Well, yes," I admitted. "And I'm the woman."

"The corpse is inside?" Derrick reached on the ground and picked up my gun; he took a whiff of the barrel. "You shot him?"

"They shot at me, I returned fire, injuring one of them in the leg. The other one escaped, firing as he did. The injured fella caught one in the chest, courtesy of his pal."

"Shit ... Okay, do you have a description of the guy who got away?"

"Sorry, no. He was wearing a mask. In fact, both of them were masked. Dark clothing, maybe six feet tall. That's about all I can tell you, Derrick."

"Who else is in the house?"

"Trevor Bowen, a coroner from Ashbee Cove."

Derrick looked at me, smiling. "You bring your own coroner to murder scenes now? Just get inside so we can sort this out. Please."

We both walked inside. The living room was splattered with blood.

Derrick noticed the bullet hole in the wall. The EMTs had already covered the body Trevor was standing by, just staring at the covered corpse.

"Trevor." He turned around. "This is Captain Derrick Edwards. He'll be handling everything from here." Trevor approached to shake Derrick's hand.

"Captain Edwards. I'm Trevor Bowen." They exchanged pleasantries.

"Monica. It appears you've got a situation. How about you two, step over here, please." He gestured for Trevor and me to step out of the living room into the kitchen. Derrick walked over to the dead guy. "You know this man, Monica?"

"No."

"Trevor?"

Trevor shook his head.

Derrick walked over to the glass slider. "They came in through here?"

I nodded.

"And you have no clue who these guys are? Maybe someone you put away in prison, Monica?"

"Maybe, Derrick. But I don't keep mental pictures of every person I put behind bars."

He shook his head while taking notes. "Two guys break into your house, both wearing masks. You shoot this guy in the leg, fire at the man who was standing near the slider, miss him, and he gets away, killing his accomplice. Is that about, right?"

"Exactly." I grinned.

He instructed the EMTs to go ahead and remove the body. "Maybe you could make us some coffee? You two have some details you need to start explaining."

"Sure, Derrick. We'll tell you everything we know." I looked at Trevor, nodding at him that we need to be cooperative with Edwards.

I was standing in the kitchen when I heard a familiar voice screaming my name from the beach. "Monica! *Monica!*" It was from Andy. He came rushing inside, almost slipping in the pool of blood by the slider.

Running up to me, he threw his arms around me. "Holy shit, Monica! I heard all the sirens, saw the flashing lights, but I thought they might be going to Mason's house. He had a stroke last week, and we had to call 911. *Ew*! All this blood everywhere. It looks like a shoot-out from the Godfather. Are you two, okay?"

"We're all right." I nodded in the direction of Derrick, who was questioning Trevor.

"Who shot who?"

"I'll explain later."

Derrick was finished questioning Trevor. He walked over to where Andy and I were standing.

"Well, I'll be damned. Officer Edwards. I haven't seen you since—"

"Since you threw that great St. Patty's Day party last year. How you been, Andy?"

"Damn good until now. Monica, I'll go get a bucket and start cleaning up all this sticky red stuff. If that's okay with you, Officer Derrick?"

"As soon as my forensic team finishes gathering the evidence."

"Thank you, Derrick, and thank you, Andy." *God bless you.*

Derrick, Trevor, and I went out to sit on the deck, carefully missing the blood pool. The sun was coming up, bringing some stability to what happened in the darkness of the night.

"Monica, Trevor. I'm going to head back to the office and put out an APB on the guy that fled, although he's probably long gone by now. I'll contact the coroner's office to see if they can get a hit off CODIS. Facial recognition might help. I just want to tell you both not to leave town. There is, of course, a whole lot more to this story than either one of you are telling me. Just get your stories straight. I'll come by tomorrow. Your facts better match and better be the truth. You got that, Monica?"

"Yes, Derrick. I promise to tell you everything tomorrow. Right now, I need to wrap my head around a few things. Trevor and I didn't lie about what went on here tonight."

"I know that. I'm sure forensics and the shells will confirm it. Still, armed gunmen don't break into a house for no reason. See you tomorrow, or the day after, latest. I'll call first."

He looked over at Andy, who was cleaning up the bloodstains on the floor. "Nice to see you again, Andy."

"Ditto, Officer Edwards. I'm sure I'll be seeing you around."

We both listened as Derrick's patrol car left. I looked at Trevor. "I don't know about you, but I could use a stiff drink right now."

Trevor walked over to where I was sitting, standing behind my chair. He started massaging my neck. "Think I'll join you." He turned to go into the house when Andy stood up from his blood cleaning.

"Okay. That's all I can do for now. The sun will dry some of it out."

"Thank you, Andy," I said. "You've been …"

"I know. You'd be there for me, too if I had blood all over the place."

I nodded and smiled.

"I think I'll join you both for that drink. In fact, you two stay put. I'll play bartender and whip up some breakfast. Don't know about you, but seeing dead people makes me hungry." He was trying to be funny, and it did lighten the mood a bit.

"You're the best, Andy. That would be very nice. Thank you."

"Anything for my queen. How about some Ramos fizzes, or Bloody Marys?"

"Andy, you can stop with the blood jokes." I looked at him with a raised eyebrow.

"Oh shit. Sorry. I was serious about B. Marys."

I smiled at his innocent intentions. "The fizzes, please, Andy."

Trevor sat back down and reached for my hand. "Sorry I froze up in there. I see blood and guts all the time ... I don't know what happened ... It's just that guy could have killed you. Shit, I should have grabbed his gun."

I squeezed his hand firmly. "I'm always ready to take down the bad guys, no matter who they are. I'm more worried about you."

He smiled. "I'll be okay. Guess when I'm in coroner mode the people are already dead when they get to me. I never witnessed anyone actually die before ... Christ. But I'm right here now, for better or worse."

"Trevor. Relax. I'll take care of everything with the police."

We sat in silence watching the dawn break, soaking in the tranquility and letting go of the horrific bloody scene that had occurred.

Andy came out, carrying a tray with our fizzes, English muffins, and fruit. "Here you go. Oh, by the way, I just got a text from Scotty. He can meet with us in a few hours. Is that okay? Might be too soon after this killing mess?"

"No, it's fine Andy, thank you."

"You two eat up and drink up. I'm going home to make a pie. I'll call you when Scotty's ready." With that, Andy took his fizz and walked back to his place, waving at the early morning surfers and strutting his little butt.

"I'm more than positive the cross is what everyone is trying to get and kill for, aren't you?"

Trevor nodded. "Agreed. Let's hope Scotty can shed some light on what exactly and why this cross is getting so much attention."

We ate and drank in friendly companionship. Despite current events and despite my fear of Trevor getting hurt, I was grateful this man was here with me in all of this.

An hour later, Trevor picked up the breakfast dishes, and I went to take my shower. The warm water cascading over my body helped to wash away the scent of blood and helped to clear my mind as to the task ahead. Scotty, with his experience in ancient relics, should be able to shed some light on our assumption that the cross was what was causing all this grief in our lives. I got out of the shower, put on a pair of jeans and a t-shirt. I could hear the shower running from the guest bath. I hoped Trevor was doing the same. Why is it that when you stand in a warm shower, all your troubles get a little more tolerable? I went to the safe and retrieved the cross. As I held it in my hands, I wondered if indeed it held magical powers. But that would be ludicrous, right?

I stood on the deck, looking at the dried bloodstains. Trevor came out the slider. He put his arm around my shoulder.

"You okay?"

I looked up at him. His eyes were so kind and reassuring. "Yes. Andy called, we're all set. You ready to meet Scotty?"

"Let's do this. Answers await." He took my hand, and we started walking down the beach towards Scotty's.

"Trevor, my heart is pounding so fast."

"Must be something you ate. Or maybe it's me?" He laughed.

I blushed. "Probably both."

Chapter 10

As we approached the house, we could see Andy waving at us from the deck. I could see the large carved stones, disbursed among impressive stone statues, echoing the professor's love of "old stuff," as Andy called it.

"Scotty is waiting for you in the library. He's getting harder of hearing and walks with a cane. I almost cried when I saw him. So speak up and clearly."

"Thanks, Andy." We followed him inside the house.

We entered the library, which was wall to wall with bookshelves, housing volumes of reference books and his own published works. Scotty was a slightly built man, with long gray hair pulled back into a ponytail. His tanned face showed the signs of a man who had been everywhere and done everything as if each wrinkled line on his face represented his distinguished career. He looked up from his desk, his rounded spectacles sitting on the end of his nose.

"Welcome. Please, come sit down. How nice to have Andy's friends in my home." His smile was that of a compassionate, caring man.

"Thank you for seeing us, Mr. Kavanaugh. My name is Monica Wade."

Trevor extended his hand across the desk. "I'm Trevor Bowen, sir."

"Please just call me Scotty. All my friends and new friends do. Of course, Andy coined me 'The Irishman,' but he," pointing to Andy, "is the only one that calls me that."

"Sir, we have something we'd like you to see. We found it at the bottom of Ashbee Cove lake."

"Yes, Monica. Andy told me a little about the problems you've been having identifying what exactly it is. May I see it, please?"

I unwrapped the cloth; Trevor picked up the cross and laid it on the desk in front of him.

"This is what we found in a watertight old steamer trunk," I said.

Scotty picked it up, feeling it with his aging hands. "Andy, could you please pour us all a shot of Middleton Pearl, please? I think we're going to need it."

"But Scotty, that's from your rare collection ..."

"Indeed," Scotty simply said. "A little history of Middleton Pearl, if I may? It was released to celebrate thirty years of this very extraordinary range of blends, a collaboration between a retired master distiller and a new master. Two casks were selected, one of a single-pot still cask from 1984 and the other a single grain from 1981. These were married together for six months in a fourth-fill bourbon barrel, which yielded only one hundred and seventeen bottles. Great care was applied in the high-end packaging and presentation. Each bottle was hand-blown in Kilkenny and laid in an oak box safely hugging the bottles.

"Andy, please pour, if you would." He had not taken his eyes off the cross.

Scotty raised his glass. "May you live to be one hundred years, with one extra to repent." He downed his shot.

Since Trevor and I didn't know any Irish blessings, we took our shots and said. "Cheers."

We could tell Scotty found it a wee bit funny. Andy was fidgeting in his chair. "Oh, for God's sake, Scotty! Start talking."

"Well, let me start by thanking you both for bringing this to me. I never thought in my lifetime that I would ever see or hold such a masterful piece, bringing closure to the speculations that the cross was a myth."

"I don't understand, sir," I said. I could tell by the way Scotty was holding the cross, that and the tears in his eyes, that whatever this was, it was a fantastic find. "What can you tell us about it?"

"Besides it being the discovery of a lifetime? It's a well-established fact that most people think the legend or myth of the Celtic cross started in the eighth century with St. Patrick. The Celtic Christian cross was claimed by Patrick to be a combined symbol of Christianity, with the sun over the cross to give pagan followers the idea of the importance of the cross. By linking it with the concept of the life-giving properties of the sun, these two ideas were to appeal to that group. Others believe that the cross on top of the circle represents Christ's supremacy over the pagan sun."

Andy spoke up. "The pagans were supposed to think the cross had magical powers that would stop their heathen ways. That's no fun."

Scotty smiled. "A clever way to put it, Andy, but as we all know that didn't work. The myth is about a young boy whose father was a hedonistic person. He killed the young boy's mother and raped his sister before killing her. The young boy thought that if he made a cross like none other and graced it with a single precious stone, his father would somehow change. The boy toiled for twenty years, making the cross. The day before he was ready to present it to his father, the father died. Distraught, the boy buried the cross and, with a grieving heart, died just hours later, leaving no sign as to where the cross was buried. Many a man believed the myth and looked for the cross with no success."

My mind was now overly cluttered with facts. "Then why was it in a metal box at the bottom of Lake Ashbee? Obviously, someone found it before I did."

Scotty nodded. "Yes. There was talk that over a hundred years ago the cross was discovered on a piece of property owned by an Englishman, after the Norman invasion in the twelfth century, when Ireland was under strict English rule. In 1922, after the Irish War of Independence and the Anglo-Irish treaty, most of Ireland seceded from the United Kingdom and became the Irish Free State. Somewhere during all of this, the cross was stolen from the Englishman and never seen again. Speculation began to surface that the cross was now in the hands of an Irishman.

"Maybe if I explain a little more about St. Patrick himself, it will help. Patrick's legendary life is an amazing story. He was born in Great Britain, to a well-to-do Christian family of Roman citizenship. When he was sixteen years old, Irish marauders came through the country, capturing and enslaving young men and women. For six years, he worked as a herder in Ireland, turning to his deep religious faith for comfort. Following the Council of the Voice (a voice that came in a dream from a prophet), he escaped his captors, finding safe passage on a ship to Britain, where he eventually reunited with his family. While in Britain, he had another dream, in which an individual named Victoricus gave him a letter entitled 'The Voice of the Irish.' He could hear the voices of Irishmen pleading for him to return to their country and walk among them. After his years studying the priesthood, he became ordained as a bishop. He arrived in Ireland in the year 433 and began preaching the Gospel, converting thousands of Irish and building churches throughout the country. He died forty years later, but not before trying to bring Christianity to the 'heathens of Ireland.' For hundreds of years, the Irish observed the day of St. Patrick's death as a religious holiday. They attended church in the morning and celebrated with food and drink in the afternoon. The first St. Patrick's Day Parade didn't take place in Ireland but in the United States when Irish soldiers serving in the English military marched through New York City in 1762."

Trevor joined in the conversation. "Scotty, what do you think this cross is worth?"

"There is no way to put a price on such an artifact. Why do you ask?"

"I want to know if it's worth the price of taking human lives."

Scotty removed his spectacles and looked earnestly at Trevor. "Yes, Andy told me about the case Monica is working. To answer your question: yes, to the right person, it would be worth killing for."

I stood up to thank Scotty. "Thank you, sir. It's been a pleasure meeting you. The information you provided is more than I ever imagined we would get."

"Monica, may I ask you who knows about the cross?"

"Just Trevor, Andy, myself and now you. Why?"

"Whoever killed that family might well have been looking for the cross; and for such a treasure, they might not stop killing until they have acquired it."

Trevor stood up to shake Scotty's hand. "We will be careful, sir. I thank you for your time and advice." He picked up the cross and wrapped it in the crimson cloth.

"Take care of the treasure you found. May St. Patrick guard you wherever you go and guide you in whatever you do. May his loving protection be a blessing to you always. Good luck, my friends."

Our lengthy visit with Scotty shed light on so many theories attached to the cross, yet left us with unanswered questions.

***

We were sitting quietly on the deck, each of us replaying in our minds the information Scotty so graciously shared.

"Now what?" Andy asked.

I looked at him. "I don't know. But if you would be so kind as to make us some of your famous bruschetta and uncork a nice bottle of wine, that might help us digest all the information we just got. Sound good to you, Trevor?"

Trevor broke his trance. "Yes, that would be great. Do you need any help, Andy?"

"Nope. I got this, Mr. T. When the queen is home, I am the indentured servant." He chuckled as he walked to the kitchen.

"What do you think, Trevor?"

"He is unequivocally a master of his craft. But I still don't get what connection the cross could possibly have with Armstrong—or Flynn, for that matter."

Andy came back with two bottles, one a 2005 Chateau Lafite Rothschild, Pauillac and the other a 2000 La Fleur-Pomerol. "Hope you don't mind me pulling out the expensive stuff. Thought we should celebrate."

"It's fine," I assured him.

Trevor picked up the Chateau Lafite. "I'm not a wine connoisseur, Monica, but I do know a little about what good wine costs. The Lafite is a little pricy, isn't it? And the La Fleur? You have some high dollars invested in these two bottles."

"I didn't purchase them. But I do have very great and generous clients."

Trevor started to uncork the Lafite. "Stop!" Andy cried. "These must be opened delicately and should breathe a bit. Were you like raised in a barn, Trevor? No offense." He laughed.

Trevor smiled. "None taken. I'm sure you're right."

"Don't mind Andy. He's a little OCD when it comes to my wine collection."

Andy went to get some of the crystal wine goblets.

"The more I get to know Andy, Monica, the more I see how worthy he is of being a trusted friend and confidant to look after your well-being."

The wine had finished breathing; Andy came out with his bruschetta, a variety of cheeses, toast rounds, and some fruit.

"This looks so good, Andy. Thank you."

"You're welcome, my sweet queen." He poured us each a glass of wine, then sat down to join us.

Trevor took a sip of the Lafite. "Very nice."

"And nice to know you appreciate good wine when you taste it," I smiled.

"You're right. I do know a good wine when I taste it. As far as anything else concerning wine, I know just enough to make me dangerous."

"Okay, you two. Enough about wine!" Andy said. "What do we do with what the Irishman told us about the cross? I say we sell it and buy an island where no one can find us." Andy was kidding, of course.

Trevor unwrapped the cross lying on the table in front of us. It was now more beautiful than ever, just knowing how old it might be and the story of who created it. "Monica, you're the pro. Where do we start?"

Andy's cell phone rang. "Hi, Scotty. Are you okay?" Their conversation continued for about three minutes.

"Is Scotty okay, Andy?"

"He's great. He started doing more research and might have a theory. He's very excited to help you and Trevor with more details on the cross."

"What did he find out?"

"I don't know. I told him I'd come over right away."

"Can it wait until tomorrow? I feel we've taken up so much of his time already today."

"Are you kidding me? The Irishman will stay up all night if he's doing research. He did it all the time when we were an item. If he says now, then it must be substantial. Tell you what, when I get there, I'll have him call you with what he found out. Will you two behave while I'm gone?"

I looked at Trevor. "Yes, we'll try."

Andy left for Scotty's with half the bottle of Lafite, which was fine since Scotty had been so gracious in sharing his vintage whiskey.

"So, Doctor Bowen, what's your take on all of this?"

"To tell you the truth, I'm more concerned about our safety. Having possession of the cross seems a little ... deadly. I feel you and I are in real danger. Plus, we've involved Andy and Scott Kavanaugh."

"You're right, of course. I think it might be safer if Andy stays with Scotty for a few days until we can get this all sorted out."

We sat and sipped, chatting further. My cell rang.

"Hi, it's me. I'm going to put Scotty on speaker and have him tell you what he's found."

I also put my phone on speaker so Trevor could hear our conversation.

"Hello, Miss Wade. Can you hear me okay?"

"Yes, Scotty, go ahead." I could tell he didn't use a cell phone much.

"I spoke to you about the St. Patrick's Day Parade in New York and its importance in the 1700s when the Irish soldiers were here. It's just hearsay, but some stories surfaced that a young soldier had unearthed something rare on a battlefield, which he brought with him to the United States. Military records show the soldier's name was Michael Barnes. After a little more research, I found that, after the war, this soldier made his way to Ashbee Cove and started a family. The time would have been in the mid-1800s. As you're aware, that's about the time the history of the Barnes legacy in Ashbee Cove begins. I also believe that, given the time span of this period, we could assume that young soldiers get together drinking and don't know how to hold their liquor. What if the young Barnes soldier told a buddy what he had found, not knowing its history or value? The story then gets passed down from generation to generation as folklore, myth, or just a legend about the obvious antics of being in the military. Could it be possible, Monica? That someone you suspect might be the killer is also an ancestor of the young friend Barnes confided in?"

I sat back. Damn! That makes sense. "I think that is a strong possibility, Scotty. That could very well be why people are dying. Thank you so much. Would you please put Andy on the phone?"

"I'm sure we'll speak again soon."

"Just me again. So how did Scotty do? Is this helpful?"

"Very helpful. I need to ask a favor, Andy. Could you stay with Scotty for a few days and do you know if he has weapons in the house?"

"You got to be shitting me. We're in danger, aren't we?"

"I don't want to take any chances. Would you please ask Scotty if there are any weapons in the house?"

"No need to ask. Scotty has a whole arsenal up in his attic, and he keeps a Ruger in his desk drawer."

"Then I want you to explain to him how important it is for you two to take some precautions. Can you do that?"

"Do you need to deputize me or something?" Even though he was making light of the situation, I could hear the fear in his voice.

"Just please stay put. I'll call you in the morning, but you need to call me if you feel something isn't right."

"Okay. I promise to look after us both. Will you and Trevor be okay?"

"We're okay. I'll call in the morning." I hung up.

"Did you find that theory of Scotty's as fascinating as I did?" Trevor asked. "What he said is entirely possible how the cross got to the US and how it ended up in Ashbee Cove."

I nodded. "It does give us a starting point. But to connect all these dots, I need to get my hands on more records on

Armstrong and Flynn. Old census records would be helpful, but ..."

"But?

"I only have limited access to confidential information with my PI license."

He smiled that gorgeous smile of his. "I might be able to help you with that."

"So, what, Doctor Bowen, do you have up your sleeve?"

"I have a friend in the FBI who owes me a favor. Would it help if I called him?"

"Yes, that *would* be helpful. You surprise me, Doctor. All this time, I thought you were just a good-looking guy in a white lab coat who kept himself locked up in a sterile environment." I smiled gently so as not to offend him.

"I guess I'll take that as a ... compliment? His name is Dean Warren. We were roommates in college for six years. I chose forensics, and he opted to catch the bad guys."

"Should we bring in the FBI? So far, we've exposed more people to the cross than we originally planned."

"Dean can get information that we can't. He will be discreet, and I trust him."

He's right. We need more outside help than I initially anticipated. "Okay, if you think he can help. Give him a call."

"Great. Dean lives in LA. Can I extend an invitation for him to come to the beach house?"

"Please do."

"I'll call him in the morning. I think we both need to get some sleep—hours without rest is not okay. Doctor's orders."

I started to get up from my chair. Trevor came over, took my hand to help me up. I was beginning to feel the full impact of these past hours, of being shot at, a dead body in my house, and knowing the other gunman was still out there. Finding out the history of the cross and worrying about Andy and Scotty being in harm's way. Standing up, I wrapped my arms around his neck, burying my head in his chest. His arms held me tight as he carried me into my bedroom.

"It's all going to be alright, Monica." Trevor took my comforter from the chair next to the bed and draped it over me. "Get some sleep, okay?" He leaned down and kissed me on the forehead before turning to leave. "Trevor, wait. I … don't want to be alone."

He walked to the other side of the bed and lay down beside me, then took me in his strong arms, cuddling me next to his body. Nothing more was said. We both fell asleep. The feeling of having him beside me was comforting, natural, and I felt safe.

Shea Adams

Chapter 11

We were awakened by my cell phone. Neither of us had moved from the comfort of each other. I turned over to pick up the phone from the nightstand. It was Andy.

"Andy ... everything okay?"

"Everything is fine. We made it through the night without anyone trying to kill us if that's what you're asking."

"Sorry ... Trevor 'n' I ... just now waking up." *Oops.*

"What do you mean you and Trevor? Is he in your bed?"

Way too early in the morning to start up a conversation about who is in my bed. "Well, yes."

"OMG, you guys are sleeping together?" The shock in his voice came through loud and clear.

Trevor was now awake. "Good morning, Andy." He was smiling.

Andy wasn't expecting to hear his voice. "Oh, yes. Morning, Trevor."

"See you later, Andy. I'm into a hot shower." He got up and grinned.

First time I heard Andy at a loss for words. "I ... um, just wanted to know what the plan is for today?"

I had to laugh. "Hey, let me clarify that nothing happened. I just didn't want to be alone last night. As far as the plan, Trevor is calling a friend in the FBI and Derrick should be coming over or calling with the information he's been trying to get on our dead guy."

"What do you want Scotty and I to do?"

"Trevor's friend might be here this afternoon. I'd like you both to join us."

"Sure. Just give me a call as to what time. I was also going to cook up some veal for dinner. I can make enough for all of us?"

"I'll call you as soon as I know. Thank you, Andy."

"Okay. Talk to you later."

I sat and thought for a while. Trevor had finished showering in the guest bathroom. I could hear him rummaging around in the kitchen. I threw on a robe and went to see if I could help him before he dismantled the cupboards. "Can I help you find something, Doctor Bowen?"

He grinned. "I was going to make coffee."

I walked over to the cupboard, above the coffee pot sitting on the counter, and took down a can of Hawaiian hazelnut coffee. "Why don't you let me make us some. I think I remember how."

"Guess Andy and Scotty made it through the night?"

"Yeah. Nobody tried to kill them, as he said."

"Is our plan still the same, for me to call Dean and invite him here?"

"Absolutely, and I should hear from Derrick soon." I poured us both a mug of coffee. "Beautiful morning. Want to sit on the deck?"

We sat down at the table and relaxed for a few moments, just looking at the beautiful Pacific.

Trevor made the call to Dean Warren. "Hey, Dean. It's Trevor. How you doing, old friend?" He chose not to put the phone on speaker, but I could understand from Trevor's end of the conversation that Dean was happy to hear his voice. They chatted back and forth, ending with why he had called. Trevor hung up. "Dean will be here this afternoon at about three o'clock."

"Great. Sounds like Dean was pleased to hear from you."

"Yeah. You'll like Dean. He's a great human being and friend." He paused to look out at the ocean.

"You know, what I don't understand is how Chief Armstrong has been able to hold his position in the department all these years. There must be people in Ashbee Cove who suspected he was crooked."

"You weren't there long enough to see the control Armstrong has over the community. No one talks about what goes on; that way, they stay out of trouble with the police."

"And how about you? Didn't you suspect something wasn't right?"

"Yes. But ... like everyone else, I love living in Ashbee Cove. I just did my job and turned a blind eye to my suspicions. Making me as guilty as Armstrong. I should have stood up to that bastard!"

"We'll make it right, Trevor. He's not getting away with murder."

I called Derrick. "Morning, Derrick, how are you …? We're fine, thanks. A little rattled but, you know how it goes. So, did you find out any more information on our dead guy?"

"I didn't find out much, not in our system. I'm looking internationally as well."

"I guess you'll be coming by today, right? Trevor has called a friend of his in the FBI. Andy and Scotty Kavanaugh will be here also."

"I'll be there. Maybe the FBI can shed some light on this guy. And you still have some explaining to do."

"We'll see you around three o'clock? Does that work for you? Andy is making dinner, so bring an appetite."

"Sounds great. Looking forward to hearing what the hell is going on."

I knew he was upset with me, that I wasn't forthcoming with him the night of the killings. Derrick had always been a good friend and was a good detective, so it wasn't fair of me to keep him in the dark. Honesty would be at the top of the list today. Not just with Derrick but everyone now involved in this case.

Trevor had gone inside while I was on the phone to Derrick. He returned with two more mugs of coffee. "What did Derrick have to say?"

"No leads on the guy I shot; not in the system."

"Does that surprise you?"

"In a way, it does. You don't just hire killers off the street. Not if you're smart. And Armstrong is."

"You still think any of this is Irish-mob related or are we just looking at a bunch of greedy cops?"

"I think this goes deeper," I said. "Deeper than the Irish mob even. It seems more and more like a personal vendetta. Just a gut feeling."

"We should know more when we can all sit down together and use our collective brains to come up with a workable scenario, don't you think?"

"I sure hope so. I want this whole case closed, and no one else getting hurt."

The morning hours went quickly, with Trevor and I taking a leisurely walk on the beach before everyone was to arrive. I still needed to take a shower and get dressed.

"I think I could walk on the beach with you from here to eternity," Trevor said.

I smiled; my heart was a little giddy. "That sounds ... nice, Doctor. As soon as we get this damn case put to bed and the bad guys behind bars."

While we walked, it was as if nothing else was going on in the world.

Back at home, I kissed him gently on the cheek and announced I was going to take a nice long bubble bath and get ready.

"I think I'll call Cari and make sure everything's okay at the office."

"If Cari needs you back at Ashbee Cove, I can handle things here."

"We'll see. Have a relaxing bath. Call out if you need me to help wash ... your back." He grinned.

Trevor joining me in a bubble bath would be fantastic! But no, not yet.

I enjoyed my bath. It was always something I missed when I was traveling to parts unknown. *Now what to wear? Do I dress down or up?* I was in the mood to get out of Levi's and t-shirts. Then I remembered an outfit I had purchased in the Bahamas at a little boutique when I was working a case in Nassau. A white pair of silk capris, white silk halter top. Paired with some Tory Burch sandals would be perfect for this afternoon. A little mascara, lip gloss, and a drop of Clive Christian Imperial Majesty. A teardrop because it's expensive, but the delicate combination of bergamot, orris, sandalwood, vanilla, and ylang-ylang extract makes it a brilliant daytime fragrance. The bottle itself was hand-blown crystal with an eighteen-carat gold collar and a diamond in the middle of the collar. My client was very grateful that I recovered five million dollars in rare gems that had been stolen from a locked safe in his home. He was eighty-five years old, and his new bride was thirty-five. He had since passed away; she was now doing time in a women's prison in California. His bride, let's just say, was now someone else's girlfriend.

I took one last look in the full-length mirror, thinking that I had aged well and could still walk the catwalk if the PI business got more dangerous than I could handle. Trevor had also changed, and Dean Warren had arrived earlier than expected and was sitting on the deck, already enjoying a beer with Trevor.

I walked towards them as they both stood up. The look on Trevor's face was priceless. Until this moment, he had only seen me in mountain clothes or casual clothes.

"Erm, Dean ... Meet Miss Monica Wade, the private investigator I was telling you about."

"Very pleased to meet you, Dean. I hope Trevor has made you feel welcome?"

"Trevor neglected to tell me how er, striking his PI was. In all my years with the FBI and working with PIs, you're the first one I've met that doesn't have a potbelly and a cigar hanging out of their mouth. Sorry, I'm sure you've heard that cliché many times." He extended his hand.

Dean pulled out a chair next to him. Trevor was still standing with his mouth open. I grinned inwardly.

"Thank you, Dean. Glad to have you here. I'm hoping you can be of some help in this case."

"Monica, can I get you a drink? How about you, Dean, another beer?" I could feel a hint of jealousy from Trevor, which was surprising but cute.

"I can get it, Trevor. You and Dean catch up." They both stood as I walked into the house.

We women know how men's voices always seem to carry further and louder than a woman's quiet whisper when talking about something private. While standing in the kitchen, I could hear every word of their conversation. I wished I hadn't.

"Well, Trevor, my man. How in the hell did you land that beauty?"

"Long story, Dean. Yes, she's a stunner; she's smart and has an elevated level of integrity, which I'm finding a bit frustrating. To be honest, we've kept our relationship professional to solve this murder case ... Christ, I'm falling in love with her! It's been a long time since these types of feelings have come to the surface. Losing Nancy and Tiffany caused me to put up a wall when it comes to getting involved with anyone again."

Nancy? Tiffany? My thoughts were wandering.

"I remember how hard it was for you, Trevor. Losing Nancy, the love of your life, was hard enough, but to lose your little girl at the same time was cruel. They didn't deserve to be taken so soon."

Oh, my God! I couldn't believe what I just heard. Trevor had been married and had a child, and they were both killed. I would think that this would have been something he might have wanted to share with the person he's falling in love with. I listened more intently to their conversation.

"I didn't think I could survive without them. That's one of the reasons I moved to Ashbee Cove. To escape the cruelty of the big city."

"Did they ever find the hit-and-run driver that killed them?"

"No, they never did. I wish I'd known Monica back then. She's a top-notch PI; maybe she could have found the asshole. I keep thinking, Dean, that she's come into my life for a reason. Not to find who killed Nancy and Tiffany, but to fill the deepest part of my soul that's been dark for so long."

"I don't know what to tell you, bud, except that I hope it works out for you. A word of advice. You need to tell her everything about your past. Keeping a secret ... not right for the path you want to take with her."

Dean was right. If we were going to move forward with our relationship, although I still wasn't sure whether there would be one, he needed to be honest with me.

I came back to join them on the deck.

Dean stood up. "You have a beautiful place here, Monica."

"Thank you, Dean."

"Do you think I should go see if Andy and Scotty need any help?" Trevor asked.

"Andy? Scotty?" Dean was looking confused.

I spoke up. "Yes, we have more people joining us, Dean. Andy is my best friend and he's being gracious enough to bring dinner. And he's bringing Scott Kavanaugh with him, a friend helping us, too—"

Dean almost spit out his drink. "You don't mean the Irishman? Is your friend Andy Weston?"

Trevor and I looked at each other. "How do you know them?"

"Interesting story. Kavanaugh was helping the FBI shut down a smuggling operation involving a museum he worked at. Andy was his partner at the time. Makes an impression, shall we say?"

Trevor smiled. "He does. And he's already become a good friend."

"Small world, Dean," I said. "I'll give him a call and see if he needs anything." I excused myself from the table and went inside.

"Hi, Andy. Trevor wants to know if you need any help?"

"Trevor said that? Oh, how sweet of him. No, I think we got this. See you in about ten."

I could tell he was bustling around, getting things together. Which reminded me: "Oh, I got a call from Derrick. He won't be joining us. Some case he needs to get to. We still have to answer questions about the dead guy in my living room. We'll go into the station tomorrow, I guess."

"Okay, my queen, see you shortly."

I walked back outside and Trevor asked, "How they doing?"

"Fine. Be here soon. Andy was very appreciative that you wanted to help." I smiled, turning my attention to what Dean was saying.

"I remember they both made an impression at the Bureau. Kavanaugh sure knows his antiquities. He was instrumental in helping us shut down the smugglers in two weeks after we'd worked on it for three years with no results."

"Why don't you and Monica tell me about this case that has you two so rattled."

"I guess you could say that we *are* a bit rattled. For some reason, some fucking assholes want us dead."

I could tell from the look on Dean's face that he was surprised at my language. Perhaps he was now seeing me as more than just a pretty face.

Our conversation was interrupted by the sound of Andy's voice echoing down the beach. The three of us stood up to watch the touching scene of Andy pulling his beach wagon filled with silver trays full of food. Scotty was walking beside him with a cane.

"Hello, hello, you all. We have arrived finally."

Trevor met them at the deck steps. "Let me help you with that pull-toy, Andy."

"I'll take care of my toy, if you would help Scotty up the stairs, please."

Trevor supported Scotty as he took the three steps from the sand onto the deck. "Good to see you again, sir."

Andy pulled the wagon onto the deck. "I'll just take all this into the kitchen." He nodded as he passed Dean, but I could tell by his expression he was trying to figure out where he knew him from.

Trevor helped Scotty to a seat at the table and introduced him to Dean. "Scotty, this is my good friend Dean Warren. He's an agent with the FBI."

Dean gave Scotty a firm handshake. "Nice to see you again, sir." It took a few seconds for Scotty to recognize him.

"Agent Warren! This is a surprise. I didn't know you knew Monica."

"Trevor and I are old college chums. I just met the lovely Monica."

"Andy told me there was going to be someone here from the FBI. I'm very pleased it's you, Agent Warren."

"Please call me Dean, sir." Dean seemed happy Scotty remembered him.

"Then you should call me Scotty. Have you had anymore smuggling cases to deal with?" He grinned.

"Just a couple of small rings we busted. Nothing compared to what you helped us with."

Andy came out of the kitchen. He looked at Dean. "Well, holy shit. Now I got it! Dean Warren! Been a long time." They shook hands.

"Yes, it has been a while. We were just talking about what a small world it is."

"Sure is. Who would have thought that you know Trevor and that we worked together on a case? Glad you're here to help. Believe me, the two Thompson Twins here have gotten themselves involved in a big old hornet's nest! Bunch of dead bodies everywhere. Shit, they even have me carrying a gun!"

I couldn't help but smile at Andy being his typical exaggerating self.

"How about we all enjoy dinner, then we can talk about the case," I suggested. "We don't want Andy's creations to get cold."

For the next hour, we passed the time with small talk and dining on Andy's excellent cooking. Andy, Trevor, and I cleared the table, leaving Scotty and Dean to visit. Andy made his famous espresso to accompany a strawberry dessert. I took the opportunity to get the cross from the safe. I joined them at the table and carefully set the crimson cloth in front of Dean.

"This seems to be the cause of the killings I'm investigating and why people are trying to kill us."

Dean unwrapped the cloth. I watched his facial expression as he looked at the cross. "What exactly is this?"

"Why don't you tell him the story of the cross, Scotty?"

Trevor, myself, and Andy could sit and listen to Scotty's articulation when describing ancient relics all day. Dean too was listening intently to every word.

"That's quite a scenario you've all put together," he said. "You seem pretty sure this is the reason for the killings."

Trevor spoke up. "It's priceless Dean, and whoever is trying to steal it thinks it has some magical power over good and evil, or so the story goes."

"What if I said, Dean, that we think these people might be associated with the Irish mob? Would that be in your wheelhouse?" I asked.

"Seriously? Why do you think these people are in with the mob?" Dean sat back, crossing his arms over his chest. "I think you guys need to tell me the whole story from the beginning."

"It all started with a phone call I received from a Steven Barnes, asking me to investigate the deaths of his brother Michael, Michael's wife, and their two children. The bodies were found aboard their yacht, The Crystal Blue, moored in Ashbee Lake near the family's summer home. I went to Ashbee Cove and procured records from the police department, under the guise that I was an attorney for the Barnes estate. I then requested documents from the coroner's office, which is how I met Trevor. I was run off the road by a black SUV, and the occupants were trying to kill me. Trevor came to assist me, and they tried to kill him, wounding him in the shoulder. Then there were two break-ins to this house, the second one ending with a dead guy in my living room and one on the run. A black SUV was found at the entry gate, which was the same vehicle, we think, that was in Ashbee Cove. The guy who escaped had to leave the SUV ... the corpse in my house had the keys in his pocket. Officer Derrick Edwards, who is a friend, and just happened to respond to the scene, is helping with identifying the dead guy. Running forensics on the SUV and ..." I took a deep breath.

"And?" Dean asked.

"I took a swim in Ashbee Lake and cut my foot on an old trunk at the bottom of the lake. Trevor pulled up the trunk. We opened it and found this cross. Then Trevor got a call that one of the witnesses who found the bodies on the yacht was found dead. There's also a woman named Johnni Flynn, who owns the local Irish pub in Ashbee Cove. We think she may be part of this, but we don't have any hard evidence. Just a gut feeling."

I could tell from the look on Dean's face that he was getting overwhelmed with information. "Let me just wrap this all up: Six dead bodies. A crooked chief of police, a few of his deputies, and a bar owner are all conspiring to kill the two of you over this cross? You do realize that this sounds like a movie script?"

Andy stood up, placing his hands on his hips. "That's what I told them, and now we're all going to die!" He started picking up the empty espresso cups. "I don't know about you three, but I think it's time for a drink!"

"I'll help you with those drinks, Andy." Trevor wanted to try and calm him down.

"I apologize for Andy's outburst, Dean. He's scared. Not for himself, but for Trevor, Scotty, and me." I reached over to take Scotty's frail hand.

"Oh, my dear Monica. You don't have to worry about Andy and me. We can take care of any problems that arise." He smiled. "In fact, you shouldn't worry about Andy at all. I'll take care of him."

The thought of those two taking care of each other was lovely but also unrealistic, if someone tried to do them harm. Although, Scotty was a tough old guy and armed to the teeth back home. *Maybe I'm underestimating him.*

"Monica, what do you want me to do? This case is more than bizarre. Sure, it *sounds* like the FBI should get involved, given the possibility of mob connections, but—"

"That's just it, Dean. I have no proof that any of this is mob-related. It's just a gut feeling, and my gut is telling me that Johnni Flynn is a major player. As far as getting the FBI in the mix, I'm just hoping you can access some information: no offense, Dean, but I would rather see if we can put the pieces together ourselves. Once we do that, the FBI will be able to take over. Besides, I made a promise to Steven Barnes, and I try not to break my promises."

"Fulfilling a promise is one thing, Monica; getting yourselves killed is something else entirely. Yeah, I can access any information we have on this Flynn and see if Chief Armstrong has any priors or connections, but that's about all I can do and not raise any red flags."

"I don't want you to put your job or position with the FBI in jeopardy."

"No, no. It won't come to that." He smiled reassuringly.

Andy and Trevor came back from the kitchen with a tray of mixed drinks: wine, whiskey, gin, and ice water.

"I didn't know what you all might want, so I brought the whole fucking bar. The water is for those of you who don't drink as much as I do when I'm nervous," Andy joked nervously.

"You need to slow down, Andy."

"Sorry, my queen. I'll behave." He sat down next to Scotty, putting his arm around his shoulder. "We'll be okay, Scotty."

"Yes, we will, Andy." He patted Andy's hand resting on his shoulder.

We all sat at the table in silence for a couple of minutes, sipping on our chosen drinks.

"Dean has decided to help us by finding out some background on Johnni and the chief," I said.

"I told Monica that I would try. That's all I can do for now. But if I see that you four are in the middle of something that might get you killed, I will get the FBI involved—whether you want that or not. Is that understood?"

The four of us were in unison with a joint "Yes."

"Then I'll start with this Johnni Flynn. Do you know if that's her real name?"

I looked at Trevor.

"That's the only name I know of," he said.

"Her name should be registered with the state if the liquor license is registered to her. I can also check with ATF and ABC to see if her name pops up. That's about all I can do at this point, in regards to her. As for your chief of police, we'll see ..." Dean pulled a small notebook out of his pocket.

I shook my head. "It still blows my mind that any woman might be involved in the murder of children."

"Money and power will do strange things to people's minds," Dean said.

"By the way, Andy. Where's Cloe?" I asked.

"Oh, she's fine. My friend wanted to keep her at his place. His little doggie has been so lonely since his puppy brother died. Cloe makes an excellent companion for Lester to play with. Which is a good thing since I don't want her in harm's way."

"Good thinking."

Dean looked at his watch. "I need to get back to LA, but it's been enjoyable and interesting."

"There's an extra guest room. You're more than welcome to stay," I said.

Trevor stood up. "You okay to drive, Dean?"

"I am, my friend or I would take Monica up on her offer. I'll be in the office tomorrow, see what I can find on these jokers. I'll call you in the afternoon. Tell your friend Derrick that I'm sorry I missed meeting him, but I'll be in touch soon."

We said our farewells to Dean. "Thanks for the help. Monica and I would love to get this all behind us and solve these murders." He gave Dean a manly hug.

"I'll do my best. You guys enjoy the rest of your evening." He left the deck, walking to the front of the beach house, where he had parked his car.

I turned to Trevor. "Dean's a very nice guy. You two must have been quite the team in college."

"My only regret is that I don't keep in touch with him. It's one of those friendships that is understood. He calls me for help, I will come, and vice-versa; it's never given a second thought."

Trevor's cell phone rang.

"Hello? Yes ... Right ... Excuse me, I need to take this call. There's been another killing in Ashbee." He walked into the house.

Andy stood up. "Did he just say there's another body?"

Chapter 12

I was stunned. Another body?

Trevor came back out to the deck. "That was Cari. They found another body."

"Who?" I walked over and took his hand.

"Debbie O'Brien."

I could see he was visibly upset. "Chief Armstrong's receptionist? Trevor that's just crazy! Why would anyone want to kill that sweet girl?"

"Exactly."

"No doubt it's Debbie?" Stupid question I realized after it came out of my mouth.

"None. Cari is looking at her right now on a cold slab in my morgue."

"I'm so sorry, Trevor. What can I do?"

"I need to go back to Ashbee Cove." He started to walk away.

"Wait, are you sure? I mean, Armstrong knows that one of his thugs is dead and the other is probably back in Ashbee Cove, which means he probably knows we're closing in on him. How much information have you told Cari about what's going on?"

"Nothing, but I can tell she knows something isn't right—what with dead bodies showing up like flies in Ashbee."

"Call her back, right now. She needs to leave."

Andy spoke up. "She's right, Trevor. Anyone remotely involved with you two will be in danger."

Scotty also wanted to help. "Your Cari can stay with us at the house. There's plenty of room. Andy and I will keep her safe."

"Or tell her to go on vacation or something," I insisted. "Get her out of Ashbee Cove, without telling her any more than she needs to know. In fact, tell her to come to Malibu on vacation—or to help you on an autopsy. Whatever it takes to convince her to leave town, all expenses paid."

Trevor sighed. "Shit, you're right. I'll call Cari back." He moved to go back inside but stopped. "Monica, are we sure this is all about the cross? That chief must have balls the size of Texas killing people in his own town."

"I agree. The truth is, though, we still have no proof ... of anything."

Trevor returned about three minutes later.

"What did she say?"

"It's all set. Cari will be leaving tonight, coming here after finishing the autopsy on Debbie. Her preliminary findings are that Debbie died of food poisoning, which caused her to stop breathing. She also said that Armstrong hasn't been asking any strange questions and, she felt, Debbie's death sincerely saddened him. No mention of either of us. I also put in a call to Mike Williams, who's stood in for me before. He's from Redding, California. He was glad that I asked him to come to

Ashbee Cove. His family needed a vacation, so I told him to stay at my place. He's unconnected to any of this, so he'll be safe."

"Good," I said. "And what about Cari now?" I noticed Trevor's hesitation. "What is it?"

"Cari ... she was very um, excited."

"Excited?"

"Yes ... To be invited to our wedding here in Malibu." A huge smile spread across his face.

"*What?!*" There are no words to explain how I felt at that moment.

Andy started his happy dance. "A wedding! How fun! *Congratulations*, you two! Why didn't you tell us that you were engaged or even thinking about getting married? You rascals, keeping it a secret! And from your best friend, Monica. How could you do that to me?

"Because I didn't know either? Until, just now!"

Trevor started laughing. "I'm sorry, Monica. But I got to thinking—"

"That everyone knows we left town together," I finished for him, working out his strategy.

"Knowing the people in Ashbee Cove, it's already been spread around that you and I are an item living in sin somewhere."

"So ... what better way for us to justify our absence?"

"Yeah, that was my thinking."

I nodded. "It will also stop Armstrong and Johnni in their tracks."

"I can call Pete Crenshaw at the newspaper and give him the announcement to print up. If Armstrong or Johnni get any ideas about fueling the fire, that we were somehow responsible for those murders and fled town, it can be put to rest. The township trusts what they read in Pete's paper."

"That's good. If I'm right about all this, Armstrong will look to pin this on us."

"Yep. Who better to blame this on? You, the beautiful stranger that came to town, stole my heart, killed the Barnes family to take their fortune. Your beauty blinded me, and we became this century's Bonnie and Clyde."

I nodded. "Only, I'm not going to marry you just to set up some alibi and draw them out into the open to close this case!"

"But Monica, *I love it!*" Andy said. "Trevor has the perfect solution to throw some shit into the mix!"

Scotty had to get his thoughts in. "They are right, my dear Monica. If you can make them think that you are both getting married, and they already know you have the cross ..."

The more I thought about this crazy scheme, the more I realized that it just might work. "All of you know how crazy this is, right? But, yeah, it has possibilities. I'll admit it's a great lure: a trap set to catch them."

Scotty leaned over and whispered something in Andy's ear. Andy nodded.

"I need to go and get something for Scotty. I'll be right back." Andy jumped the three short steps from the deck to the sand and ran down the beach towards Scotty's house.

Scotty motioned for Trevor to come close. He then whispered something in his ear. Trevor responded with a smile.

"Okay, can you let me in on the whispering?"

Scotty smiled. "Andy will be right back, then you will see."

It was beyond me what these three were conspiring. But in my experience, when three men get together and start planning something, it can't be good.

Andy came back a few minutes later, out of breath from running back to the beach house. "Okay, I'm back. Trevor, Scotty, come inside with me, please."

Trevor went to help Scotty up from his chair, and they went inside, leaving me standing by myself with no explanation except for a "We'll be back in a second, my queen. Just stay put."

I could see them inside, giggling as if they had all just inhaled some laughing gas. Andy and Scotty came back first, sitting at the table. Then Trevor walked up to me and proceeded to kneel on one knee. He opened a small box, pulled out the most beautiful emerald ring I had ever seen. Taking my hand and looking deeply into my eyes, these words came out of his mouth.

"Miss Monica Wade, would you do me the honor and accept my humble proposal of marriage? Monica, will you marry me?"

My knees started shaking as he held my hand tightly. I smiled at the thought that this ruse had gone this far, so I went along with the fantasy. "Yes, I will marry you, Trevor." Andy and Scotty stood up and started clapping. Trevor stood up, took my face in his hands, and gently kissed me.

"Wait up! Enough is enough, you guys. Remember this is a sting operation. Trevor and I aren't really getting married, but the sentiment you pulled together was very sweet. And where did you get this ring, Andy?"

Scotty walked over to where I was standing with Trevor. "My dear Monica. I purchased this ring years ago when on a dig in Ireland. One of my colleagues and I went into town one afternoon. As I walked past this antique store, I saw this ring displayed in the shop window. It was so brilliant, majestic, and alluring I just had to have it. I knew one day the ring would be destined for someone special. Today is that day. I'm honored that it's you."

"Scotty, I can't keep the ring. This is just pretending. Trevor and I aren't really getting married."

"I understand, Monica. Still, the ring will symbolize your strength together and help you bring these murderers to justice. Please keep it as a gift. You will make this old man so happy."

"I don't know what to say, Scotty." I gave him a hug and a kiss on the cheek.

Andy joined our little threesome. "Stop all this love stuff; we need to decide what to do next. It's obvious I'm the only one here capable of planning the perfect wedding. I'll take care of everything. It'll be a killer wedding ... Oh, sorry! Poor choice of words. Anyway, first, I'll call my friend Ivan. Do you remember him, Monica, the professional photographer who took that photo of Cloe and me for our Christmas card last year? We'll need a picture to send to the Ashbee Cove newspaper. Right, Trevor?"

"Right." Trevor was finally coming out of his gaze, which was fixated on me and the ring.

"I think this little fantasy of yours, Trevor, might just work." I smiled.

"If we want justice for Michael, Sarah, and those two innocent children who were brutally taken from this world, I think it's worth the risk."

"Okay, then. Let's do this." I gave Trevor a strong hug of approval.

I looked at Andy. "Go call your photographer friend and see if he can come by this evening. I think a sunset engagement photo would fit the bill."

"He'll be here, I promise. Now, what are you two going to wear for the photo shoot? I suggest all white and barefoot on the sand."

I just shook my head and smiled. "Whatever you think, Andy."

"I know you have that fantastic white cotton Vera Wang in your closet, Monica. It would be perfect. Trevor, do you have any white cotton pants or a white dress shirt?"

Trevor was looking confused. "Ah, nope."

"No worries. Give me your sizes, and I'll go shopping."

One of Andy's gifts was his style. He would find the exact outfit for Trevor to complement my Vera Wang.

Andy walked over to where Scotty was sitting. "Scotty, I'll walk you home, then go shopping for Trevor. Is that okay with you?"

"Yes, Andy. I need to get some rest. It sounds like I'll need it to keep up with all of you!"

We watched as Andy carefully guided him as they walked arm in arm back to his house.

Trevor took my hand as we stood watching them. "It'll be okay, Mrs. Bowen."

I punched him lightly on the arm, his good one. "I sure hope so, Doctor Bowen. Seriously, though, I don't want anyone else hurt. Why don't you go call Crenshaw at the newspaper and give him a heads-up, and have you thought about what you're going to say when you call Chief Armstrong?"

Trevor looked at me, shaking his head and shrugging his shoulders. "I'm just going to pretend that everything is cool and say I'd like him to attend the wedding?"

"I can't believe he would be that stupid as to accept. Surely, he's smarter than that and could recognize a setup."

"Maybe. But I'd wager he brings some of his Irish friends. They'll be out of sight, but he'll make his move. No question about it."

***

My cell rang. "Okay, my queen. Ivan just called me back and said he looked at his bookings and didn't realize he had a photo shoot tonight for some commercial. Good news, he has tomorrow completely open and will be on call. You need to decide if you want a daytime shoot or go with the sunset idea. Either way, he's cool. More good news, I found the perfect outfit for Trevor."

"That's fine, Andy. Tomorrow will be okay. I think we need a break tonight anyway. Are you staying with Scotty tonight?"

"Yep. We'll be getting the guest quarters ready for Little Miss Cari."

"Thanks. You and Scotty relax, as well."

Trevor came back out to the deck after calling Pete Crenshaw. "Who was on the phone, Andy?"

"Yes. We have to postpone the shoot until tomorrow. Which leaves us the rest of the evening to decide on exactly what to tell Chief Armstrong."

Trevor could tell I was starting to feel like the "runaway bride."

"Monica, you need to trust me. Pete is on board with running the article and helping any way he can. He also said the town's starting to get nervous with all the dead bodies showing up. The delay will give us time to get our plan ready for catching Armstrong and Flynn."

The rest of the day and early evening was spent discussing the "wedding." I pulled all the files from Ashbee Cove, going through them again to see if there was anything we might have missed. I went over again with Trevor what he first found and what we later found on the Crystal Blue. With witnesses and co-conspirators dead, not one bit of proof, all we had were our theories and gut feelings.

I sighed. "I don't know about you, Doctor Bowen, but I need to get some sleep."

I took his hand and led him into the bungalow. He must have gotten the impression that he was going to be a guest in my bed as he started to follow me down the hallway. I turned to him and kissed him on the cheek. "I'll see you in the morning, Trevor." I went into my room and shut the door. I'm sure with disappointment he did the same. I needed time to regroup my thoughts on the day's events, and why I was letting Trevor take such control of this case. All the decisions, the ruse of creating a fake wedding ... I needed my head in the game. But it wasn't there. And I knew why.

Both my bedroom and the guest room where Trevor was staying had ocean views with a private deck. I got into bed and stared out at the amazing creation outside my window. The vast Pacific Ocean was there to greet me each morning and wish me sweet dreams at night. I was blessed to live in such a beautiful place. I fell asleep to the ocean's gentle waves.

Chapter 13

Waking up to the warm sun dancing through the window, I cleared my eyes, watching as a familiar profile was walking up to the beach house. I quickly threw on some sweats and a t-shirt to greet him.

I stepped out onto the deck just as Trevor was walking up the steps. "Good morning, Doctor Bowen. How was your walk?"

Trevor looked surprised. "Oh! It was awesome. Where's your coffee?"

"I'll get a cup in a minute. How did you sleep?"

"Amazingly well. Not hard to go to sleep with the sound of the waves as your lullaby." He smiled. "How about you?"

"Fine, I guess."

"Sit down and relax. I'm getting a refill, so I'll make you a cup."

"Thank you."

He returned with our coffees and pulled a chair next to me so we both could enjoy the ocean view. He took my hand in his, giving me a reassuring squeeze. "So, we shoot at sunset?"

"Yes, I think that's what Andy has planned."

"What's wrong, Monica? You seem a little distant." Trevor put his arm around my shoulder, pulling me closer to him.

My cell phone vibrated on the table, allowing me to escape from Trevor's question.

"Good morning, Andy."

"Good morning to you, my queen."

"What's up?" I took a sip of my warm coffee.

"Well, Ivan would like to start setting up the photo shoot about four o'clock this afternoon. Is that okay?"

"That's fine, sweetie. What about Trevor's outfit? Do you need him to come to you for a fitting?"

"Of course not. I've got Trevor all set, and it will be perfect. Okay then, see you around three o'clock with some munchies for the crew."

"Crew?" I was a bit confused.

"Yes, dear, the crew. We must set the scene. Don't worry your pretty little head. I've got this."

"Of course, you do. I'll see you later, and thanks for all the work you're doing to pull this together. Bye."

Trevor gave me another gentle hug. "Sounds like our engagement is underway. You still seem a little on edge. Share with me what's going on in that head of yours."

"Nothing. Just bear with me, please. This is the first time I've ever been engaged, let alone getting married. Plus, I feel like I'm giving you and Andy too much decision-making. This is my case! If someone gets hurt, it'll be my fault. I understand that you have all the best intentions when it comes to helping me and you need to bring the Barnes family closure. The only reason I'm going along with this outrageous plan is that you know Armstrong better than I do. If this gets out of hand, Trevor, I'm pulling the plug. Understand?"

Trevor stood up and walked to the deck railing, staring out at the ocean. He turned and motioned for me to join him.

"Monica, you're right about bringing closure to this case and holding Armstrong responsible, and whoever else is involved. If you think it's a bad idea, just tell me, and we'll find another way."

"No, the plan is good. But I feel some underlying reason why you want justice so badly. Do you think it's because of what happened to your wife and daughter?"

"What? How the hell ...?"

"I've known since your friend Dean was here. I was getting our drinks and I overheard your conversation about their deaths. I'm so sorry, Trevor."

"Why the hell didn't you say something sooner? I've been dealing with all this guilt about not telling you!"

I moved closer to him. "I knew you'd tell me about them in your own way, in your own time. I can't imagine what you must have gone through. This is not something that you casually bring up in conversation. I totally understand."

Trevor was silent for a few minutes. I didn't want to push the subject, which I'm sure was very painful for him. He turned to me with tears in his eyes.

"Monica, I'm sorry about not telling you from the very beginning of our relationship."

"It's fine. We don't have to talk about it at all."

"Yes, we do ... I-I want to ... Nancy and I met when we were both grad students at Stanford. I was studying forensic science, and Nancy was getting her master's and a doctorate in bioscience. I fell in love with her the moment she walked into the lab, where I was working on a cadaver. She didn't even flinch at the sight of a dead body being dissected. We started dating, both finished getting our degrees, then decided to get married. The wedding was small, with just a few friends and family attending. Nancy was the kind of woman that was easy to be with. You remind me of her: strong, caring, and beautiful ..."

I smiled but looked away, shy.

"Two years later, she was pregnant with our first child. A precious little princess named Tiffany came into our lives. Tiffany was the best baby two novice parents could ever have. We moved to San Francisco, where I became the chief medical examiner. Nancy chose to be a stay-at-home mom, putting her career on hold until Tiffany was older. Then, one day, Nancy was out shopping with Tiffany. They wanted to get me a special gift for my birthday. On their way home, a car ran a stop sign as they were crossing the street. He hit them going fifty miles an hour, in a twenty-five-mile-an-hour zone. They never had a chance ... Both were killed instantly on impact. The driver fled the scene and was never caught. That's when I quit my job in the city and decided to take the coroner's job in Ashbee Cove. The town was small, quiet, and I just needed to breathe. That was over eight years ago."

I could feel his pain and anger. "Trevor, I don't think the pain is supposed to go away when you lose someone you love so much."

"Monica, look, I-I don't want you ever to think that there isn't room in my heart for you."

His comment started me thinking: Was I ready to get into a committed relationship? This whole engagement thing was just a plan to bring Armstrong out into the open and throw his ass in prison and get him to take responsibility for all the murders in Ashbee Cove. I cared for Trevor very much. But a lifetime partner? A ringtone on my cell interrupted my thoughts.

"Hello, my sweet queen, who's almost ready to be a blushing bride."

"Oh, hi, Andy. How are you?"

"Well, from the sound of my queen's voice, better than you are. What's up?"

"Nothing, Andy. It's ... We're okay. You'll bring Trevor's clothes?"

"Of course, unless you want him naked in the photos. I already told you! I've. Got. This. Covered." Andy was trying to lighten up my mood.

"How much time do we have before Ivan arrives?"

"A couple of hours. I'm on my way now, because I know it will take me time to make sure everything is perfect."

"I'll start getting ready. You can oversee Trevor."

"My pleasure!" Andy laughed.

"Trevor, that was Andy. We've got a couple of hours before the shoot. I'm going to start getting ready. Andy said he would take care of you."

Trevor put his arms around me. "Are we okay, Monica?"

I kissed him gently. "Yes, we're okay. Thank you for telling me."

He smiled, though it didn't reach his eyes.

"Hey, let me go make myself look like someone who just got engaged!"

I broke Trevor's hold and went inside, leaving him to wait for Andy, who was already walking down the beach towards the bungalow, his arms full of garment bags and dragging his beach wagon behind him, full of "goodies" for the crew.

***

I stepped into the shower, letting the warm water caress my body. I reached for my favorite bodywash, foamed up the loofa sponge, and traced every inch of my skin, enjoying the delicate aroma of coconut. There was a knock on the door.

Please let this not be Trevor. Not right now.

"Monica, do you need any help getting into that Vera Wang?"

Hearing Andy's voice put a smile of relief on my face. "No, thanks! You just concentrate on Trevor."

"Roger that."

I listened as he closed the door behind him, then finished my shower, adding some coconut oil to my skin and catching a glimpse of my naked body glistening from the glitter in the oil. Not bad. I opened the satin cover to reveal my Vera Wang, which had been hanging in my closet since my last trip to the Bahamas. The skirt was white cotton, with a slit up the side. The top was off one shoulder and cropped just below the bust line. It was the pure elegance that I so loved about her designs. My bronze tan against the pure-white cotton would make a good contrast for the photo. Now, what to do with my hair? After trying a couple of twists and pinning it up, I decided that going with my hair's already natural waves would be best; plus, it was less work than trying to blow out my long, thick hair. A little blush, lip gloss, and a dab of perfume would complete my task of looking like a bride-to-be.

When I came out of the bedroom, I could hear all the commotion going on outside. Apparently, Andy's crew had arrived and were like busy little ants setting up lighting and a white arch covered with greenery and fresh flowers on the beach. As I stepped out onto the deck, I saw Trevor, who was dressed in slightly baggy white cotton pants, a white shirt, unbuttoned halfway down and the sleeves of the shirt cuffed. He looked very handsome. Someone grabbed my waist from behind.

"Well don't you just look like a million bucks, my queen. Damn girl, you've still got it! I mean, look at all those body parts still in their right places. Oh, and I love the hair. Just relax girlfriend. It won't hurt a bit." Andy smiled and blew me a kiss. "Hey, what do you think of Trevor's outfit?"

Trevor turned around at the sound of Andy's voice and walked towards me. "I don't have anything to say, except that you are breathtaking, Miss Wade."

I was a little embarrassed. "Not bad yourself, Doctor Bowen."

Andy came up to Trevor. "I just need to borrow him for a second, Monica. I promise to bring him back." The two of them walked a few feet away, Andy whispering something in his ear.

Trevor came back over to where I was standing. "Andy said they should be ready in about fifteen minutes. They want to get the perfect shot just as the sun sets. Apparently, Andy and Ivan have it timed down to the second."

He poured us each a margarita out of a glass pitcher that had been put on a table surrounded by munchies for the crew.

"I don't think they'll miss these. Do you?" He winked and pulled out a chair for me to sit down.

We just sat and watched as the crew, Ivan, and Andy put on the finishing touches.

"Andy's done a magnificent job. Is he always this detailed?"

I grinned. "This is nothing. Wait until you go to one of his parties. Andy is very well known in Malibu for his extravagance. People pay him a good chunk of change to be their party planner."

Trevor chuckled. "Andy works?"

"He doesn't have to work; he's worth a few million." I liked the shocked look on Trevor's face.

"Maybe I need to treat Andy with a little more respect."

I looked around the deck for Scotty. "Trevor, isn't Scotty coming?"

"Andy said he was feeling a little tired, told him it was okay just to stay home and rest."

Andy came running up to the deck and over to the table. "Okay, people, it's *showtime!* Just go sit down under the arch. I have a white satin blanket for you to sit on, and there are two full glasses of red wine. I want you to gaze into each other's eyes. In other words, act romantic. And please don't spill the wine. Now, get down there, please, before we lose the sunset."

We followed Andy's instructions. Ivan and his crew were ready for the lights, so we sat down on the satin blanket, looked at each other, and smiled. Then something happened.

"I love you, Monica," Trevor said quietly. "How would you feel about making this real? The engagement and the wedding." The words came flowing from his lips.

My heart was beating so fast. It almost scared me. I didn't know what to say, except. "I love you too, Trevor. Yes, I will marry you." *Did those words just come out of my mouth?*

Trevor leaned over and kissed me as if he had never kissed me before.

I put my head on his shoulder. Lights were flashing, cameras clicking, the voice of Ivan saying, "Good, very good ... Give me more ... Perfectly stunning, you two."

Then the shoot was over ... Trevor and I were in a trance.

"Hello, hello ...? Earth to Trevor and Monica."

I looked up. "Don't tell me we have to do this shoot again, Andy." I was blushing.

"On the contrary, my queen and king. It was *marvelous*. Ivan will be back with the negatives in a few minutes. He's old school, no digital, but with the set up in his van he can do the prints on the spot. Then all you have to do is pick one out." Andy was looking at us strangely. "What the hell's up with you two? Did a sand crab bite you in the ass?"

Trevor took my hand in his and smiled at Andy. "We're getting married." He pushed me over onto the blanket and wrapped me in his arms.

"Yes, Andy, we're getting married!" I chuckled.

Andy was looking at us like we were both nuts. "Of course, you're getting married. Isn't that the plan?" Then he looked at my face. "Holy shit! You guys are getting married for *real*?" He sat down between us on the satin blanket and joined us in a group hug. "When, why, how did this happen? This is *awesome*! But now I need to find a real preacher."

Trevor helped me up from the blanket, holding me tightly. "I'd say you better jump on it, Andy, before this beautiful woman changes her mind."

"Shit, I guess so! A beach wedding, yes?" Andy started doing his happy dance again.

In all the excitement, I started doing my own happy dance with Andy as Trevor just stood by smiling.

"Crap! I need to go tell Scotty. Wait! Monica, I just thought of something. I don't need to find you a preacher man. Scotty is an adorned minister. Well, kind of. It's a mail-order thing, but it's legal. He got his license a few years ago so he could marry some of our gay friends. What do you think?"

I looked at Trevor, who nodded. "I would love to have Scotty marry us," I said.

Andy started running down the beach towards Scotty's. "He's going to be as fucking surprised as I am!" His arms were waving in the air.

Trevor and I started walking back to the bungalow, then he suddenly stopped and swooped me up into his arms and carried me up the steps to the deck.

"Well, that was special, but you can put me down now!" I gave him a kiss on the cheek.

"No can do, Monica. I'm never going to let you go."

"So, you're going to carry me to the bathroom? I need to pee!" I laughed.

Trevor shook his head and grinned. "You are a stunner, Monica, but sometimes what comes out of your mouth amazes me."

"You'll get to know me, Doctor, and understand that there are many, many times what comes out of my mouth is either amazing or just plain trash."

"One of the things I love about you. You have the face of an angel and the spirit of the devil; throw in a couple of bikers, a convoy of truckers—pretty much sums you up."

"Hold that thought. But I really need to go pee." I went inside, making it safely to the bathroom. I stood motionless, looking at myself in the mirror.

Monica Wade you just accepted a proposal from Trevor! I'd never been married before; I just hoped the whole marriage thing came with a book of instructions.

I heard Trevor call out, "Can I fix you a drink?" He called out from the hallway.

I flushed the toilet, washed my hands, and opened the bathroom door.

"Sure! A cold glass of iced tea would be great, but I'm going to change first."

"Need any help?" I heard him laugh.

"Slow down, Lone Ranger. We're not married yet."

I quickly changed into some shorts and a tank top. I pulled my hair back into a ponytail and joined Trevor, who was sitting at the table with our drinks ready.

"From supermodel to tomboy. I like it." Trevor handed me my glass.

I raised my glass. "Here's to you getting to know the two different sides of me."

Trevor raised his glass. "And here's to me loving whoever you are at the time. I do recall meeting one side of you that was an attorney. Is that what you're talking about?" He wore a cocky grin.

"Okay, let's change the subject from me to how we're going to lure Chief Armstrong, Johnni Flynn, and his henchmen to the wedding. Secondly, what about the cross?"

"Like I said before. The chief's ego won't let him pass up the chance to get his hands on the cross. Do you have any ideas in that crafty brain of yours, Miss Wade?"

Random thoughts were racing through my head. "We could make it part of the wedding ritual. Maybe have it on display as a symbol of our love."

"That's an expensive gamble, exposing it to everyone at the wedding, don't you think?

"What everyone? There's you, me, Andy, Scotty, and Cari. Dean and Derrick will be undercover, and they could stand by as if they were part of Ivan's photo crew. Still, you're right: that's eight people. Plus the catering staff we're putting in danger."

"Do you not want some of your family and friends here to share in the joy of your wedding?"

I turned and took his face in my hands. "Sweetie, I don't have any family or friends. I was adopted, raised an only child, and my adoptive parents died when I was fifteen. I don't have many friends because I don't trust people, nor do I have the time or energy to foster real friendships. Except for Andy. Which is perhaps why we're so close. What about you, is there anyone you'd like to invite?"

"Since you're asking, no one. I have everything and everyone I need right here."

I felt sad that we didn't know much about each other. "Your parents, siblings?"

"I have a brother, Adam, who's a world-renowned heart surgeon; he lives in France. My sister Anna is a pediatric trauma nurse and resides in Australia. My mother and father passed some time ago. The three of us were raised by a wealthy spinster aunt, who spoiled us rotten and left her vast wealth to be divided equally between us and a small stipend for her two cats. The last time I talked to Adam or Anna was fifteen years ago at her funeral."

The more we shared, the more I realized that Trevor and I had more in common than most couples who had known each other for years before jumping into the wedding pond.

My cell chimed. "Hello, Andy."

"Did I interrupt you, my queen?"

I smiled at Trevor, mouthing the word Andy. "No, you didn't. What's up?" I put the phone on speaker so Trevor could listen in.

"Ivan has the prints ready for you to look at. They're gorgeous, just simply *gorgeous*! The two of you together just makes my heart melt. Anyway, I'll rush them over so you can pick out the one to fax to the newspaper. I took the liberty of writing up an accompanying article about your engagement. But, my darling, you haven't set a date for me to add to the article. Did you and Trevor decide yet?"

"Come on over. I'll discuss it with Trevor. See you in a bit."

Chapter 14

"Well, what do you think?" I asked my fiancé. I could hardly believe that I was discussing my wedding day!

"We need enough time to contact Armstrong and extend our gracious invitation," Trevor said. "So, if we fax the photo to Crenshaw today, it'll run in tomorrow's edition. I already mentioned it'd be coming."

I started counting the days on my fingers. "Today is Friday. The article breaks on Saturday. You can call Armstrong on Monday. We can set the wedding date for next Sunday. Do you think that'll give us enough time?"

"I'm sure the chief will clear his calendar." His remark carried an overtone of disgust.

"And Flynn?"

"I thought of that. The chief and Flynn are tight, which I assume means she will be coming with him."

"I think it'd be better if you call her and extend a personal invitation. After all, she's a love interest from your past." I shrugged my shoulders.

"First, she wasn't a love of mine; just maybe in her mind, she was. Secondly, if she did have any part of killing those children, she needs to be strung up by her thumbs."

"We know that she was in contact with the guys in the black SUV that tried to kill us, which by coincidence is registered to her. And I think Johnni is up to her tight little ass in everything remotely involved with the murders. Maybe she's the mastermind behind all of this. We really don't know. I'm also a firm believer in keeping your enemies close."

"You're the boss, and you're right. I'll make the call this afternoon, using the premise that I wanted her to know about our pending wedding rather than read it in the newspaper. In fact, I'll do the same with Armstrong."

"Perfect. Now, my soon-to-be hubby, we're on task." I gave him a quick kiss just before his cell rang.

"Hello, Cari." He hit the speaker button.

"Hi, Trevor. I'm sorry, but I won't be able to attend the wedding. My brother was in an awful car accident and is in critical condition. I need to fly to Florida and be with him and his family. His wife Rhonda is ready to give birth any day. I hope you understand."

"Oh, that's awful! I'm so sorry to hear, Cari. Of course, family always comes first. Is there anything I can do to help?"

"No, thank you. I have my ticket and will be flying out on Sunday."

"We understand, Cari. Monica and I will be keeping you and the family in our thoughts. Keep us updated on your brother. You stay safe."

"To tell you the truth, Trevor. Any place is safer than Ashbee Cove, under these circumstances. I'll keep in touch.

Thanks again for understanding. I'll be thinking of you and Monica on your wedding day. So excited for the two of you. She's a catch! Hold her tight and don't let go.

"I will. Bye." Trevor ended the call.

"One less person at the wedding." He seemed disappointed.

"Remember why we invited Cari here in the first place—to keep her safe."

We saw Andy walking up the beach with Scotty holding onto his arm.

Trevor helped Scotty up to the steps onto the deck.

"Good to see you! Andy told me the good news—that we have a wedding to plan. A real one!" He came over and gave me a hug.

"Yes, we do, Scotty," I laughed.

"I'd be humbled to officiate at your wedding; I assure you both it's all very legal." A wide grin spread across his aging face.

"Thank you, Scotty." Trevor shook his weak hand.

Andy placed several photos on the table in front of us. "Time to pick your pic."

"Which one do you like, Andy?" Trevor was now standing behind me with his arms around my waist.

I snuggled into his embrace. *Gosh, this feels so right.*

"You want *me* to pick one?" He placed his hand on his heart.

"You're the one with the creative eye." Trevor gave him a smile.

"Well, then, I would pick ... this one." He held up a photo of Trevor and me, wine glasses in hand, gazing into each other's eyes. The sun was just setting, and it did look magical.

"Shall I fax it to the paper?"

"To Crenshaw, yes, please. The number is on my desk by the fax machine."

"On it, my queen and king." He went inside.

We joined Scotty at the table. Trevor hoisted the umbrella since the glare from the sun was in Scotty's eyes.

"Thank you, son. That's much better. Do you mind if I ask you what the plan is for catching these outlaws?"

"Scotty, can I get you something to drink. Iced tea, a glass of wine?"

"Tea would be very refreshing, Monica, thank you."

"Trevor, can I get you anything?"

"A cold beer sounds good. Thanks."

"You can catch up Scotty on our ideas about the cross."

Andy had just finished faxing the photo and cover story to Crenshaw.

"We're all set. It looks like sherry time. Remember those blueberry scones I brought over. If there are some left, I'll make up a tray with that delightful blueberry jam that lady gave you. The sweetness paired with the sherry would be exquisite."

The story behind the jam was kind of interesting. One day, while doing some paperwork outside on the deck, I saw this little lady walking her tiny dog on the beach. I watched as this four-legged, white ball of energy broke away from her hold on the leash and headed for the water. The woman was in distress, calling for her beloved companion to come back. Like crooks, a dog when called rarely stops running, unless he's very well trained. Long story short, I was able to leap into action, retrieve the dog from drowning, and comfort the little emotional lady. She was so grateful she showed up at the bungalow the next day with homemade blueberry jam.

"Did you come up with a plan yet?" Andy asked as he placed the sherry, in its delicate antique crystal decanter, on the table.

"That's what we're going to do right now, Andy. I'm not worried about the wedding. I know you'll have that tightened up top to bottom. We just need to figure out how to bring the cross into the scene.

"I'll go get the cross out of the safe. Did you change the combination after the break-in?" he asked with his mouth full of a blueberry scone.

"No need. First break-in they didn't find the safe. The second break-in the assholes didn't have time because ... well, one of them died."

"Good point." Andy went to get the cross.

Trevor looked at me, cocking his head to one side, with a questioning look as to why Andy would have the safe's combination.

"I trust him with my life and everything in it." He understood.

Andy returned, laying the cross on the table, unwrapping it from the crimson cloth. The four of us said not a word. We just stared at its beauty.

"Okay, guys, we need to decide," I said, breaking the reverie. "Do we let everyone see it, or do we keep it under wraps and make them try and find it?"

Scotty spoke up. "What if I have the cross sitting on the Bible when I have you repeat your vows?"

Andy, Trevor, and I looked at each other, answering in unison, "Brilliant idea!" We all smiled at Scotty.

Andy got up and gave him a hug. "You're just so smart, my friend."

Scotty blushed.

I took the cross in my hands and held it up to the sun's rays. "Do you really have magical powers?"

My question was rhetorical, but Scotty said, "Remember the cross indeed has powers to those who, in their illogical minds, have heard the stories passed down from generations before them. The fact that Chief Armstrong and Johnni Flynn might have a distant connection to one another through family and are determined to possess it, plus are willing to take human lives in the process ... well, that does give the cross powers, in a sense."

"A genuine and costly sense," Trevor added.

"The monetary value of that thing is not a bad reason, either." Andy was pointing at the cross as if it was an evil, possessed object.

"I agree. These factors will be why they show up. So, we need to take precautions. They've been responsible for all the unexplained deaths in Ashbee Cove, and they will kill again. Trust me." Trevor was right in being so concerned.

I wrapped the cross back up in the crimson cloth as if to hide it from hearing what we were saying. "So how do we protect ourselves?"

"Derrick and Dean will be here with guns, right?" Andy gulped down his second glass of wine.

Something was spinning in that brain of his. "What are you thinking, Andy?"

"I was just thinking that they need to be as close to us as possible with those big guns they'll be carrying. Why not make them your best men, Trevor? I'll be Monica's maid of honor and will be walking her down the 'aisle of sand.' It's not like we'll have fifty people here. This would keep us all together and safer. Don't you think?" He was nervous, I could see.

"There might be a slight problem with that idea. We'll be like sitting ducks if they bring any heavy firepower with them."

"You mean like the fucking Irish mob, don't you?" Andy stuffed another scone in his mouth.

I stood up, looking around at our enclosed environment. "Do you see all the places here that a shooter, or shooters, could hide without being seen?"

Andy came and stood beside me. "Crap. I didn't realize we were so vulnerable. Big rocks, cliffs, the road on top. Lookout point. Damn, they could hide anywhere! *Shit!* How do you think we'll all look with a bulletproof vest under our wedding attire?" Andy was trying to be funny, but it wasn't that funny.

"First, I need to make a call to the chief and Flynn," Trevor said. "We haven't even thought about what to do if they don't show up." He made a good point. "I'll go make them."

"My queen, we need to get you a wedding gown."

"I want this to be a casual affair. A traditional wedding dress is out of the question. How about palazzo pants and a tank top?"

"Let me think about it. The palazzo's not a bad idea; the tank top is out."

Andy and I continued our banter about what I should wear.

"Appears we're all set. Both Armstrong and Johnni will be at the wedding; they even thanked me for calling before they read it in tomorrow's edition! In fact, Armstrong said he was honored to receive an invitation. Johnni wasn't sure about coming until I mentioned the chief had already accepted. I even suggested they could possibly drive here together."

"Excellent job, Trevor, my man. Looks like I need to get busy. I have a 'killer' of a wedding to plan. Ready to go, Scotty?"

Scotty steadied himself on his feet. "It will be a beautiful wedding day, Monica and Trevor. We will all be fine."

We watched as Andy and Scotty disappeared. Trevor pulled me into his arms, giving me a gentle kiss. I could feel my heart beating against his muscular chest. My body was quivering with desire. All I wanted at that moment was for him to make love to me. The response I felt from his body told me he was feeling the same. We both knew what was going to happen next as we started walking towards the bungalow, but suddenly Trevor stopped.

"Monica, are you sure you want to do this?"

The passion I was feeling became fear. I was starting to think that I might be the bride left at the altar in the sand by the runaway groom. "Do I want to marry you or do I want to have sex with you? Because the answer to both questions is yes."

"I'm sorry, what I'm trying to ask is, would it be better if we saved our passion for our wedding night? I want it to be the most memorable night of your life."

"Trevor, you do know that I'm not a virgin, right?"

"But you will be my virgin bride, and that needs to be extraordinarily enchanting and even more magical than you can ever imagine."

I threw my arms around his neck, just held onto him as tightly as I could. "I'm so lucky to have you in my life. I've never been happier than I am this very moment. I love you and will love you forever."

We held our embrace until my cell rang. Placing a kiss on Trevor's lips, I answered the phone.

"Hey, gorgeous. How are the two lovebirds doing? You guys 'nesting' yet?"

"Oh, funny, Andy. If you could only be a fly on the wall right now."

"Sorry, queenie. Voyeurism isn't my style. But you two just get all the nasty you want."

"For your information, Trevor and I have decided to wait until our wedding night to consummate our relationship."

"Get out! Really?"

"Why did you call, Mr. Weston?"

"I don't want to bust that romantic little bubble you're in, but remember that there will be killers lurking around your perfect day." His voice was higher pitched than usual.

"Thanks for the update, Andy. You're apprehensive, aren't you?" I needed to take his feelings seriously.

"I'm sorry, yes ... I'm scared shitless but am so happy at the same time; you, my forever queen, are finally getting married! I just want it to be perfect and wish this whole thing could be done differently. How about we just give them the fucking cross and call it even?"

"I wish I could, Andy. But I made a promise to bring the people responsible for the Barnes family murders to justice. I know you understand how important this is. I'll check in with you later." He ended the call.

Trevor came back from making his calls to Dean and Derrick. "What did the 'men in black' have to say?" My voice was edgy.

"What's wrong, Monica?" He wore a face of concern.

"I just got off the phone with Andy, talking about how beautiful it's going to be. He reminded me that there will be killers here, probably hidden behind bushes with guns. It just popped my romantic bubble back to reality. Not how I imagined my wedding day."

"Dean and Derrick are already on top of things, and none of them involve the use of bulletproof vests as part of our wedding attire." He gave me a hug, patting me on the back like he was burping a newborn.

"I'm sure they can handle any situation that comes up. I still have this gnawing feeling in my gut that Armstrong and Flynn have been plotting their plan long before the wedding. This just gives them a chance to move it up a notch …"

***

The week seemed to go by quickly. Trevor and I visited the cop station and spoke with Derrick. We didn't have to get our accounts "straight," as Derrick had asked us, as, of course, what went down was precisely as we both said. Besides, the ballistics results were done, backing up that we were exactly where we said we were inside the house.

I'd been through this kind of thing many times before, so it was all pretty much routine for me. For his part, unlike the night it all went down, Trevor was calm and methodical in his account, every bit the professional who worked with law enforcement.

Derrick thanked us and said that, barring any further details they might need to dot the "I"s and cross the "T"s, it was fine, pending getting the body ID. We signed our statements and went off for a delightful lunch at a little deli I loved. I thought, as we ate and chatted, how well Trevor was merging into my life. Soon I'd be Monica Bowen, PI. That would take some getting used to after all these years of being Wade. But I'd be Mrs. Monica Bowen, wife … That already felt good. Safe. Oh, not jobwise—that was not an issue since I'd been handling cases, some dangerous, for years. But that balance I'd been coming to realize I had lacked for so long. To fully be with someone; to want to simply *be* rather than *do*. With this man. Yes, Mrs. Monica Bowen would enjoy that.

Meanwhile, as the week progressed, Andy was making all the wedding arrangements, including my outfit, caterers, music, and flowers. I don't know what I would have done if I had to do this myself. Trevor received a call from Chief Armstrong stating that he and Johnni had come in a day early and were staying at a hotel in town and were looking forward to the wedding tomorrow. My ass, they were looking forward to it.

Armstrong and Flynn, along with a few of the entourage of killers, no doubt, had checked into the National Hotel, a quaint little out-of-the-way place in the hills above Malibu with a panoramic view of the Pacific Ocean. Its discreet, private surroundings were once known as a hangout for some of the movers and shakers of the Hollywood elite. Sadly, over the years, it had lost its luster, with only a few small rustic cabins that were rented out.

Still, it made the perfect location for Armstrong to plan his assault.

Chapter 15

Chief Armstrong and Flynn sat at the bar, sipping a couple of beers, talking about their strategy for tomorrow's event. Milo was tending bar. A slightly built man, in his late seventies, with coal-black hair, which one could quickly tell had been dyed, Milo had been at the National from the beginning, and anytime you went in, he was happy to share the hotel's history with anyone willing to listen.

"Then our plan is clear. A few of my guys will be in a fishing boat about a quarter-mile offshore with MK17s equipped with laser scopes." Armstrong reached for a napkin and pulled an ink pen from his shirt pocket. He started to draw a diagram of the road above Monica's bungalow.

"Can I get you another beer?" Milo approached them, wiping the bar with a stained white towel.

"Sure." He dismissed Milo's friendly attitude and continued talking to Flynn.

Johnni looked at the scribbles on the napkin. "Don't you think that's a little risky? What if someone spots them?"

"I had one of the guys check it out. The road is lined with large boulders and eucalyptus trees. No way they will be seen." He gave her a pat on the shoulder. "Getting cold feet, Johnni?"

"Fuck you, Armstrong, you're out of line. If it weren't for me, you wouldn't even be in Ashbee Cove. You wouldn't have known that we're fucking related and sure wouldn't know the history of the cross and the importance of getting it back to its rightful owners. Which is us, asshole." She looked around to see if anyone heard them. The bar was empty, except for Milo washing some glasses at the end of the bar.

"Oh hell, Johnni, calm down. Don't forget who recruited Barnett and Ryan to do your dirty work." He slammed his fist on the bar, which caught Milo's attention.

"Everything okay here, folks?" He put fresh cocktail napkins under their beer glasses.

Johnni smiled. "We're okay, just some sibling rivalry."

"Are you staying here at the National? It sure has some history, this old place." Milo grinned, thinking this was an opportunity to get a conversation going.

"Yes, we are." Johnni looked at the name tag, hanging crooked over his shirt pocket. "Milo."

"Well, you came to a great little hideaway. Not many visitors anymore. Not like the good old days when the place was in its prime. We'd have movie stars, politicians, musicians, singers, and the big bands. This was the place to be seen." He wiped off the bar again with the same stained towel.

"Sounds interesting. How about a couple more beers?" Armstrong interrupted.

Johnni turned her barstool around to face him. "You do realize this is probably a setup. Monica Wade is no idiot."

"That bitch has no clue what I'm capable of doing." He grabbed her wrist. Nor do you."

"We need to make sure everything is timed perfectly if we're going to pull this off," she sneered, breaking his hold on her wrist.

"It will be. Once everyone is dead, we grab the cross and get the hell out of there. I've planned for a private plane to take us across the border. From there, we board a cruise ship to Guatemala, hang out for a week or two, then head to Ireland. I have a buyer for the cross, and then, dear cousin, we'll be set for life."

They weren't aware that Milo was taking mental notes of their conversations; nor that he was a good friend of Andy Weston and thus his connection to Monica Wade. He approached them, holding two more beers in his hand. "I need to take care of something in the back. Will you two be okay until I finish up? These beers are on the house." He set the beer glasses in front of them.

Flynn sensed something was wrong. "Do you need any help? I own a pub where we're from. Those cases can get pretty heavy."

Milo didn't make eye contact. "No, thanks. I can manage. You just enjoy your beer. I'll be back in a few minutes."

She watched him start towards the back room, picking up his cell phone near the cash register. "I don't like this," she whispered to Armstrong. "I'm going to see what exactly he has to do in the backroom that is suddenly so important."

Armstrong shrugged his shoulders. "Whatever, but I think you're getting paranoid."

Flynn followed Milo to the back room, but when she opened the door, there was no one in the stock room. Just cases of beer and a few bottles of hard liquor. She opened the back door leading outside and saw Milo talking on his cell phone.

Milo was calling Andy, but it went straight to voicemail. "Hey, Andy. Can you give me a call when you get this message? Something strange is going on here at the National that you need to know about ASAP. Call me back."

Milo saw Johnni approaching out of the corner of his eye and pretended to continue talking. "Jerry, you jerk. I thought I told you to bring me twenty cases; I only counted ten. Get me those other cases here by this afternoon." He pushed the end call button and put the cell in his pocket.

"Hi, Milo. Problems? I was coming out to get some fresh air and get away from that asshole brother of mine. Distributor issues?"

"Yep. You know the business; they just can't get the orders right."

"Why don't you give me your phone and I'll make sure you get your cases. I'm pretty good at putting pressure on these guys."

"That's okay. This happens all the time, and they will make it right eventually. I need to get back inside. Ladies first." He motioned for Flynn to go ahead and back inside. As they entered the stock room, Flynn quickly eyed the cases of beer and counted twenty.

Armstrong grinned. "You and Milo have a good time?"

"Milo was making a phone call. He said it was a distributor, but he was lying."

"Who do you think he was talking to?"

"Monica Wade, for all I know." Flynn was not happy.

"Milo?" she called. "Would you bring me another beer? This one's warm."

Milo nodded, then poured and brought her a cold beer.

"You've been around here a long time, right? Do you happen to know Monica Wade?"

Milo looked directly at her. "I've heard the name. Why?"

"She was in Ashbee Cove not too long ago and came into my bar. We chatted a bit; she said she was from Malibu, I recall."

"I don't know her personally." He picked up some limes and started slicing them on a cutting board.

Flynn continued to drill him. "Malibu is a small community. Surprises me you haven't met her before. I think she's some famous private investigator."

"Nope, haven't had the pleasure." He continued slicing and stacking the limes in a stainless-steel container.

Armstrong got off his barstool. "Johnni, we need to get back to the room. I have some paperwork to finish up." He placed two twenties on the bar as a tip.

"Thank you, sir, that's very generous of you."

Flynn was still sitting when Armstrong grabbed her arm. "I said, let's go. I have things to do." She pulled away.

"Nice talking to you, Milo. Hope to see you again before we leave, and I hope you get that order straightened out."

Milo watched as they left the bar. He finished wiping up the lime juice that had squirted onto the bar, then saw Johnni come back in. "Did you forget something?"

Johnni walked behind the bar. "You're a lying piece of shit." She grabbed the knife before Milo could react to defend himself and plunged the sharp blade deeply into his stomach with an upward thrust.

Milo fell to the ground, gasping. He jerked and gasped some more before letting out a last raspy breath.

Flynn dragged his lifeless body into the back room and behind some cases of beer.

"Maybe you need to go back to school, Milo. You don't count very good." She looked at the bloody knife in her hand, returned to the bar, washed it clean, placing it back on the cutting board. She then opened the cash register and took out the money. Whoever would find the body would think there had been a robbery. Flynn wasn't worried because no one had seen them in the bar.

She walked back to her room, found Armstrong standing outside, waiting for her.

"Did you grill Milo some more?" he asked with his stupid grin.

"Shut up, Cullen. I need some rest. You go hang with those thugs you brought along." She opened the door to her room, but Armstrong blocked her.

"Those thugs are going to make us rich. You really can be a bitch, Johnni."

She pushed him aside and slammed the door, then proceeded over to a mirror hanging above an old wooden dresser. She looked at her reflection, brushing the mane of red hair from her face. She smiled. "You have no idea just how big a bitch I can be, Chief Armstrong. You have no idea."

Shea Adams

Chapter 16

That unique ringtone on my cell only, set for Andy.

"Hey, girl."

"Hi, Andy. Bet you've been working your ass off getting everything ready. Sorry, I'm not much help." My voice betrayed some of my guilt.

"You need to stop worrying so much. I'll have my crew start setting up about four-thirty tomorrow. That will give us plenty of time to have Derrick and Dean check out the area. They aren't going to let anything happen to any of us or ruin this day. Is it too late for Scotty and me to come over? He's written a beautiful ceremony and wants to go over it with you. Is Trevor there?"

"He took a walk … but I see him coming back down the beach."

"Perfect. We'll be there in five." Andy disconnected the call.

Trevor stepped onto the deck, removing his shoes. He knocked the sand off on the railing.

"How was your walk, Doctor?"

"Invigorating as always, Miss Wade. Plus, it gave me a chance to get a little better idea in my head as to what the area looks like around the other houses and the road coming into the Colony. There are a few places someone could hide, but not many, which gives me a little more confidence." He walked over, giving me a good-morning kiss.

I smiled. "Andy called. He and Scotty are on their way over with some ideas about the ceremony."

Trevor put his arms around me. "Are you still worried about tomorrow?"

"Of course, I am. Are you saying you're not?"

He smiled. "Maybe a little concerned. But I still don't know how Armstrong and Flynn can steal the cross and leave without being caught."

"These two have been able to cover up all the murders without anyone suspecting them and have gotten away with it."

"Monica, come sit down." He pulled out a chair at the table on the deck. "They won't get away with it again. Derrick and Dean will make sure they spend the rest of their pathetic lives behind bars or, better yet, be put to death for their crimes." His voice was strong.

"You're right. I'm going in to make a cheese tray for us. Would you like to make a pitcher of your martinis? I'm sure Scotty and Andy will enjoy something refreshing."

Trevor stood, reaching his hand down to help me up but, unexpectedly putting me in a dance hold, he began twirling me around the deck. At that moment, I knew we were going to be okay and that my decision to marry this wonderful guy was the right one.

I sliced some imported cheeses, opened some caraway seed crackers, and arranged them on a gold platter as I watched

Trevor shake up his martinis. "Do you know how many years we'll have to be married to have a golden wedding anniversary, Trevor?"

Trevor thought a moment. "I believe that's fifty years, Miss Wade. Why?"

I smiled. "Because I want to be with you for our golden anniversary. Of course, that would mean we'd be over one hundred years old!"

Trevor laughed. "We might be in wheelchairs, but we'll be together, I promise."

I wrapped my arms around his neck, and we were starting to kiss, when our romantic interlude was interrupted.

"Okay, we're here, so break it up in there!" Andy helped Scotty sit down, then looked up at me. "Oh, no. Monica, you've become a domestic diva! You made cheese and crackers all by yourself!" He laughed. "I'm impressed."

I gave Andy a hug, then Scotty, before pulling a chair up close to him. He took my hand.

"Good evening, my dear Monica."

"I'm so happy you're here, Scotty. Andy said you've been working on the ceremony?"

"Indeed, I have. The words came easily because of the love you and Trevor share for one another. Where to display the cross ... that was a little more difficult. Are you sure you want it as part of the ceremony?"

I looked at Trevor and Andy, already enjoying their martinis. "Yes, Scotty."

Trevor finished swallowing the cracker and cheese he had just put in his mouth, followed by another sip of his martini. "I believe that it needs to be in view, yes."

Andy raised his hand. "I procured an elegant pedestal to be placed under the arch of flowers. We could put it on there."

I thought for a moment. "Do we really believe that the chief or Flynn are just going to walk up, steal it off the pedestal in front of everyone, and casually walk away with it? I don't think so."

Scotty spoke up. "Monica's right. The cross should be visible during the ceremony, but then taken back inside or displayed on a table during the reception. I'm not a thief, but I think that's when they'd make their move."

Andy put his hand on his heart as he looked at Scotty. "You are just so smart, my friend."

I sat back in my chair. "Of course, you're right," I agreed. "But then we're putting all our friends in danger. What if they start shooting up the place? Andy, do you have a headcount on who will actually be here tomorrow, including your crew?"

"Ivan plus four, those are his lighting people. Three will be here from the Flower Attic. I invited them to stay after setting up. Four from the little band 'Staircase.' You'll love their music. Six from Devon's Catering. Derrick and Dean." He looked at Trevor. "How many other men in black will be with them. Did they say?"

"Two more of their guys will be joining them, but will be positioned up on the main road, above the Colony entrance."

"Okay, I count twenty plus, which includes the two "assholes" Armstrong and Flynn. So, let's say thirty, just in case a couple more show up."

I shook my head. "So many for a small, intimate wedding."

"It's your wedding day, my queen. It's a small group considering my reputation as the best event planner in the world."

"I'm just thinking over this whole situation and the danger."

I got a pouty face in return. "Maybe we should just think positive and try to enjoy the day. It's your wedding, Monica." He crossed his arms over his chest.

Trevor stood up. "Aren't we missing the point here? We need to catch them in the act of stealing the cross. Neither Dean nor Derrick can do much if a crime isn't being committed."

Andy came out of his pout. "I say we hang them by their feet over an open bonfire."

"May I make a suggestion?" Scotty chimed in. "We know that the cross has some personal value to them besides its monetary worth. I can start talking about the cross during the reception. Surely, they'll be interested in my findings as an anthropologist?"

"Excellent scenario, Mr. Kavanaugh." Trevor nodded his approval.

I gave all three of them a smile and raised my martini glass. "Here's to finally getting justice and closing this case."

"I don't know about you two, but Scotty and I need to get home and make sure everything is ready for tomorrow. Monica, I have your dress, which I will bring over in the morning, and your ensemble as well, Trevor. Since I'm going to be the 'maid of honor,' I took the liberty of buying myself something appropriate and charged it to your account, Monica." Andy gave me a chuckle

"Dress? Really, Andy? I thought we agreed not a dress." I gave him my distinctive "look" again.

"Oh, just relax, my queen. You're going to love it and be the most beautiful bride to ever walk down the aisle—or sand, in this case." He came over, gave me a hug and a peck on the cheek. "See you bright and early in the morning. Now, you two lovebirds go cuddle, or whatever people do on the eve of their wedding."

I had to laugh. "See you tomorrow. Thanks again for all your help, Andy, Scotty."

Trevor helped Scotty down the stairs and onto the sand. Once again, the two walked hand in hand across the beach to Scotty's bungalow.

"You think they'll stay a couple, this time?" he asked me. "Seems their love and caring for each other is heartfelt."

I leaned on the deck railing, smiling at the two of them. "Maybe. At one time, I thought Andy had found his soulmate when he met Scotty. But there is the age difference and Scotty's failing health."

Trevor comforted me. "This is all going to work out. There will be a happy ending. I promise. Now, you and I are going to take Andy's advice and go cuddle." We walked into the bungalow and into my bedroom. "Slip into something comfortable. I'll make sure everything is locked up and be right back."

I started thinking about the promise we made to each other: no sex until our wedding night. Was that about to change? I put on some flannel boxers and my baggy t-shirt that says "Born in the USA," which I had gotten at a Bruce Springsteen concert.

Trevor returned to my bedroom, wearing some flannel sweats and a t-shirt proclaiming Stanford University. We looked at each other and started to laugh.

"Lie down, Monica." Trevor pointed to the bed.

"But I thought we agreed to wait?"

Trevor put his fingers to his lips. "Shhh."

He took the comforter from the foot of the bed and covered me, then crawled in beside me. Slipping his arm under my back, he drew me towards him. We were now facing each other. I could feel my heart racing.

"Close your eyes." He kissed my forehead and whispered, "It's just cuddling … so, no taking advantage of me. Goodnight, Monica Wade."

I was both relieved and disappointed at the same time. "Goodnight, Trevor Bowen."

We fell asleep in each other's arms.

Shea Adams

Chapter 17

I didn't dream, which is unusual given what would be happening in just a few hours.

Trevor was already up and making fresh coffee, and I could smell something sweet. I liked the feeling that gave me, the man I loved being in the kitchen.

I got out of bed, washed my face, brushed my teeth, and ran a brush through my hair. I saw Trevor standing in front of the stove, cooking.

"Good morning, Doctor Bowen. Whatever you're cooking smells great."

"Good morning, Miss Wade. Grab a mug and go relax on the deck. I'll bring my creation out and join you."

I poured myself a mug of coffee and walked out onto the deck to enjoy the early morning sunshine and the sound of the waves saying good morning to the sandy beach. Trevor set our breakfast on the table.

"This looks and smells delicious, Doctor. What have I done to deserve this?"

Trevor winked. "It's what you *will* do, Miss Wade."

I took a bite and was delightfully surprised. "Mmm, Andy would love this!"

"I have a few hidden skills that you don't know about. Besides, Andy told me that if I didn't know how to cook for myself, I would probably starve to death. Just think that in a few hours, we will be Mr. and Mrs. Are you ready for today?" He smiled.

"You mean getting married or bringing down Armstrong and Flynn?"

He laughed, trying to break the tension of his question. "Both. Mostly becoming Mrs. Monica Bowen."

"I'm sorry, Trevor. I didn't mean to slight the fact it's our wedding day."

"I know you didn't. I've thought about it a lot. That maybe we should have waited until after we take care of Armstrong and Flynn. But I don't want to wait for you to become my blushing bride. Today will be the start of a new life for us both."

My cell made the Andy tone. "Happy wedding day, my queen! How are you doing this morning? Nervous as a 'whore in church'? Just kidding!"

"We're doing fine. Just having breakfast."

"OMG, you didn't cook, did you? I mean, you maybe should have waited until after the wedding to show Trevor you have no abilities in the kitchen."

"Stop it, Andy! It's my wedding day. Today of all days you need to cut me some slack. Besides," I chuckled, "Trevor did the cooking."

He laughed. "Thank goodness someone in this new arrangement can prepare food."

"We will always have you around, Andy, to be with us and hopefully make sure we are well-nourished."

"Ah, that makes me want to cry, but I won't—not yet, anyway. Okay, be there in ten with your wedding gear and Trevor's." He ended the call.

I looked at Trevor. "Andy will be here in ten with our 'gear,' as he's now calling our wedding outfits." I smiled, knowing that Andy would always be with me. *Just as Trevor will.*

"Let's try and keep this as a traditional as we can, shall we? Meaning I can't see you in your *gear* before the wedding."

"Cute!" I said, rolling my eyes, thinking this is going to be anything but "normal."

Trevor pulled up a message on his phone. "Dean. He'll be here in an hour."

I started pecking out a message to Derrick. Within seconds of receiving my message, there was a return text: *Hi, Monica. Be there within the hour. I am in touch with Dean. He should be there at the same time.*

"Appears Dean and Derrick have been communicating. Derrick will be here with Dean."

We were enjoying the ocean when we heard a familiar voice.

"Permission to come on deck?"

There was Andy at the foot of the steps holding his "gear" bags. He was dressed in white khaki pants and a pale blue dress shirt with ruffles down the front. He turned in a circle.

"So, what do you think? Is this perfect for a bridesmaid's outfit or what?" he chirped.

Trevor and I looked at each other and gave a thumbs-up.

"You look amazing," I said. "Thank you for being here with us."

"No, my queen and king, the honor is all mine. Ivan will be here in two hours for pre-wedding photos, so make sure you're ready, please."

Trevor looked at Andy. "But Andy, I'm not supposed to see the bride in her wedding *gear* before the wedding. Right?"

Andy put his hands on his hips. "Well, I think it's okay if we make an exception, in this case, Doctor Bowen. Given that nothing else is 'trad' in this wedding." He rolled his eyes. "Well, I need to help Scotty get ready, so get dressed together or apart, whatever blows your skirt up. Chop, chop, my friends!"

We watched Andy do his famous saunter down the beach, chatting with everyone he saw. *It won't surprise me if half the vacationers on the beach get an invite to the wedding.*

"Appears the boss has spoken." Trevor unzipped his gear bag. "Interesting."

"What is?"

"Never mind. A bride can't see the groom before the wedding." He winked. "Aren't you going to look at your gear?"

"No, I'm not looking at my 'gear.' How the hell did this 'gear' thing get started, anyway?! See you later, Doctor." I gave him a queen's wave with my hand.

The warm water felt good flowing over my body, calming my hidden nerves. In a few short hours, I would be married to a man I'd only known for a brief time. Although I felt that fate had brought us together to make this journey, I also couldn't help thinking the worst: Just what were Chief Armstrong and Johnni Flynn planning?

***

The parking lot was void of cars except for the rentals that Armstrong had rented for his hitmen. The National was utterly vacant of guests, so it seemed likely that Milo wouldn't be found until after they were well on their way to Mexico.

Flynn had just gotten out of the shower when she heard a loud knock on the door to her room. She wrapped herself in a towel and opened the door. "I like the fresh look, Johnni." The chief was leaning against the door jam, his eyes tracing her partially nude body.

"Keep your fucking eyes in their sockets, Cullen. We aren't kissing cousins, and never forget it. You try anything and I'll cut your balls off, understood?"

"Settle down. When will you be ready to go? I'm sending the guys ahead to set up their vantage points. The boat is already offshore with the Wade bungalow in their sights." He straightened up to expose his dress blues.

Flynn looked him up and down. "Is that what you're wearing. Your uniform?"

"Can you think of a better way to avoid being spotted as a thief?" He chuckled. "No one will suspect the chief of police in dress blues to be a criminal."

"Whatever, Cullen." Flynn slammed the door in his face. Opening her suitcase, she pulled out a long green backless dress, simple in style but acceptable for a beach wedding. Her figure was tight, her skin flawless, and her flowing red hair set off her emerald eyes. She was pleased with how she looked in the mirror. There had been few opportunities in Ashbee Cove for her to show off just how beautiful she was. She packed her suitcase, then went around everything she had touched in the room, taking a damp towel to make sure no fingerprints were left behind. She hoped Armstrong and his goon squad had done the same. Shutting the door behind her, she saw Armstrong standing by the car.

"Did you remember to clean the rooms?" she asked.

Armstrong opened the trunk and threw her suitcase inside. "Of course, we did. This isn't my first rodeo, Miss Flynn. By the way, you look stunning! Don't think I've ever seen you dressed up before." A sinister smile crept across his face as he opened the passenger door. "Miss Flynn."

They drove away from the National Hotel, following two of the shooters driving a red Corvette. Armstrong's thinking was that, while they might question a black SUV with blacked-out windows, no one would suspect a Corvette parked in the exclusive area of the Malibu beach homes. This would also allow the shooters to make a quick exit after the chaos began. He took his time driving to the Colony. The red Corvette passed them to take position. He pulled his car off the road at a sign that read "Lookout Point."

"So, this is it." Flynn opened her car door, stepping out to see the view. She turned to Armstrong. "I sure hope your guys don't get spotted before the ceremony starts."

"My God, Johnni. These guys are pros. They know what they're doing. Trust me, will you, please?"

"Cullen, this will take perfect timing. One mishap and we're done. Do you understand how critical this is? I'm not ready to go to prison, and you sure as hell wouldn't make it inside more than twenty-four hours once they find out you're a cop. After the first shot is fired, we'll have the whole Malibu sheriff's department responding."

Shaking his head, he went and opened the trunk of the car, pulling out a pair of binoculars. "Look." He handed them to Flynn.

"Look at what?"

"Look out beyond the row of beach houses, about a quarter-mile. What do you see?"

"The fishing boat with four of your guys on board."

"Exactly.

"Sounds like you've covered every possible scenario, Cullen. I apologize."

"My guys are good at what they are hired to do: kill." He smiled at being one step ahead of her thinking process.

"I hope so." Flynn looked out at the ocean.

"Just remember our goal is to cause confusion long enough for us to steal the cross and get the hell out."

Flynn knew it wasn't going to be that simple, but arguing with Armstrong at this point would be futile.

***

I unzipped the garment bag Andy had given me. It was no surprise that he had picked out the perfect outfit for my wedding day. I smiled because it wasn't a dress. It was an off-the-shoulder, white-cotton jumpsuit. He had included a small blue-feathered hairclip instead of a veil. We weren't wearing shoes, so he put in a blue and gold toe ring.

Andy was such a romantic. Simple yet elegant. I was happy.

Trevor was ready and waiting on the deck, dressed in his white pants and pale blue shirt. He watched as I stepped onto the deck from the bungalow.

"What do you think, Doctor Bowen?"

Trevor approached. "I do believe you are the most beautiful bride that will ever walk this earth." He gazed into my eyes, holding my hands in his.

I gave him a once-over. "Not bad yourself, Doctor. I like the blue shirt; it matches the blue feather in my hair." We both smiled and gave each other a hug.

We sat and watched the commotion that was beginning to take place. Ivan arrived with his crew of photographers. The caterers arrived to set up on the deck for the reception, and the florist came with baskets and baskets of fresh flowers: daisies, blue roses, white roses, potted blue and white hydrangeas to display around the deck, and finally, a white lattice arch with climbing fragrant jasmine intermixed with white and blue roses to be placed on the sand. A white satin runner was put from the deck steps, across the sand to the arch. Andy had outdone himself again.

My cell phone chimed. "How are the queen and king doing?"

"Well, Trevor and I are dressed and watching all these clever little ants running around getting everything ready."

"Isn't this just as exciting as hell? Scotty and I will be there shortly. I want to make sure everything is just the way I want it. Ivan will be taking pictures of you both, so make sure you've got your beautiful, sexy self altogether and please make sure Trevor leaves his shirt unbuttoned a little, and the cuffs on his shirt are rolled up two turns. Got it?"

"Got it, maestro. Smile, be sexy, shirt open, cuffs rolled—two turns." I disconnected the call.

Trevor smiled. "Orders from the boss man?"

I nodded, smiling, giddy like a teen with her first crush.

Andy was right. Ivan approached with his camera and a couple of his lighting crew. "Are you ready, guys? Would you please follow me down to the beach? I'd like some shots by the water."

Ivan was a total professional and knew what he wanted. At the end of the beach is a famous rock formation that looks like a heart. Since the beach in front of the bungalows is considered private, very few people get to view it. It's become a popular spot for photographers, and Ivan used it often in his work. I knew his photos would be amazing. We finished with Ivan, just as Andy and Scotty were arriving.

Andy greeted Ivan with a hug. "How'd they do?" he asked, pointing to Trevor and me.

"They made my job easy. Can't go wrong with these two. Every shot ... quality. I might have them both sign a release so I can use the photos in my advertising." Ivan gave us a wink.

Scotty was sitting quietly at the table on the deck. He saw me approaching and stood up. "Monica, my dear. You do look enchanting." He reached for my hand.

I curtsied. "I believe I finally feel like a bride-to-be, Scotty."

He grinned. "It appears Andy has completed his vision as to what your wedding should be. I hope he didn't overstep any boundaries."

"Scotty, you've known Andy a very long time. We both know boundaries don't work with him! No, everything is just how I imagined it would be. Maybe not as lavish as he would want—but perfect. Ah, I see Dean and Derrick have arrived. Will you please excuse me a moment?"

Trevor was already talking to them as I walked up. "I see my top G-men are here to make sure my wedding is uninterrupted."

"We've been here since early this morning, checking out the area. So far, nothing stands out as suspicious."

I noticed Derrick wasn't smiling.

"Then ... what?" I asked him.

"I need to speak to Andy. There was a murder at the National. Milo the bartender was killed. We found his cell phone; he called Andy shortly before he died."

"Oh, my! Not Milo ... He's part of the furniture here ... Wonder why he called Andy?"

"Exactly. Excuse me."

***

Derrick found Andy talking with the catering staff.

"Andy, hi. Great spread. Listen, did you get a call from Milo yesterday?

"No. I haven't talked to Milo in months. Why?"

"I'm sorry to have to tell you ... today of all days, but Milo was found murdered at the National. We found his phone at the scene, and your phone number came up as last dialed."

Andy's face dropped. "Oh, my God. Poor Milo. Who would want to kill that loveable man?" Andy bent slightly, breathed deeply.

"So you didn't get a call?"

"Let me check my phone. Maybe I missed it. I've been running around like the Roadrunner for the last couple of days ... Oh, shit. He did call me. And he left a message. Christ! Let me put it on speaker ..."

"Andy ...? Andy! You there? Shit. You have to call me back. ASAP."

"Why would he call me?"

"That's my question. You have no idea why he would have called?"

"No. Oh, God ... I wish I'd answered. Do you think ... Is it my fault Milo is dead? Maybe he needed help? Damn, I can't believe I missed his call! And now he's ..."

"It's not your fault, Andy. I've got detectives working on it. It could have been a simple robbery, gone bad."

"Does Monica know about Milo? She doesn't need any more death on her mind. Let's not address this right now, please?"

"Yes, Andy. I told her. But you're right. Enough is enough for today."

***

"Derrick's right," Dean said. "It would be difficult for anyone to try and hide near the beach and bungalows. We even went door to door, unofficially, making sure the residents in the houses were supposed to be there. A couple of them questioned us on why we were asking, but we just said there was going to be a wedding and we were private security. They accepted it like it wasn't unusual to have private weddings on the beach. We also have one of our guys operating the security gate. Have you heard from Armstrong or Flynn?" Dean looked at his watch.

Trevor's cell made a "*swoosh*," indicating a text message. He looked at his phone, then up at the three of us. "Speak of the devils ... they'll be here shortly."

"We know what they're here for—and it's not the food, booze, or to wish us good luck. Scotty will be officiating, and the cross will be on top of the Bible, which will be sitting on the pedestal in front of him."

"Good. I don't think they'll make a move until the reception. This means the two of you will be able to exchange your vows and get married. There'll be a lot of people roaming around on this small deck after the ceremony. Derrick and I'll be in constant communication with each other." He pointed to his ear.

***

Armstrong pulled up to the security gate. "Chief Armstrong and Ms. Johnni Flynn for the Wade wedding." He showed the guard his ID.

"Yes, sir. Please drive ahead to the end of the road. There is a valet who will park your car." He pushed the button to retract the gate.

Flynn looked at all the beautiful bungalows as they drove to the end of the road. "Monica must be making some big green to be able to afford this area."

"It's my understanding she's at the very top of her game. Too bad she won't be able to spend any of it," he chuckled.

A young valet approached the car. "Good day. Your keys, please, sir."

Armstrong was hesitant to hand them over, even to someone as cute as this girl. "We'll be leaving early. Do you mind if I park the car where we can get it when we're ready to go?"

"Of course, sir. If you would kindly pull to the right side of the road, I'll make sure you aren't blocked in."

"Thank you, miss. Appreciate it." He backed the car to a spot, making their exit easy.

He and Flynn got out of the car and walked to the bungalow, where they were greeted by another young woman, this one holding a tray filled with glasses.

"Champagne? Please follow the pathway around the side of the bungalow."

Flynn and he both took a glass from the tray.

"You do realize this is a trap," Flynn said. "They will have security here. How are you going to handle that?"

"No problem," Armstrong assured her. "As soon as I spot them, I'll signal our shooters to hit them first. With them down and people scattering, it'll be easy to grab and go."

Flynn simply nodded.

***

The pathway around the side of the bungalow was well marked with potted plants. Andy had given instructions for the young hostess out front to text him when Armstrong arrived. I looked over and saw Andy look at his phone. I turned to Trevor.

"Appears our guests have arrived."

Trevor signaled Dean and Derrick. "Shall we go greet our guests, Miss Wade?"

We both moved to the middle of the deck and watched as Armstrong and Flynn came around the corner of the bungalow. I couldn't believe my eyes when I saw Johnni Flynn. She sure didn't look like the same woman I met at the bar in Ashbee Cove. I noticed even Trevor was trying to figure out if it was the same Johnni Flynn.

Trevor extended his hand to Armstrong. "Glad you could come to the wedding, Chief. Nice to see you, Johnni."

"Thank you for inviting me, Trevor; this is an extraordinary day for you both."

Johnni was being friendlier than I remembered. She gave Trevor a hug.

"And sweet Monica. You are a breathtaking bride. I was a little surprised to hear that you and Trevor were getting married so soon after meeting. But I think love works in mysterious ways sometimes. Besides, time waits for no man, or woman, eh? I figured something was up when you didn't return to Ashbee Cove. Looking at your beautiful place here, I don't blame you for not coming back to our small town."

I despised that she was talking out her ass; all her sly innuendos made me sick to my stomach. I was searching my mind for a proper response other than slapping her in the face.

"Yes, Johnni, I think we were both surprised, too!" I simply said, thinking again how this bitch was about to get the shock of her life. "Trevor and I need to go talk with my wedding coordinator, please excuse us for now." I took Trevor's hand, and we strolled over to where Andy was standing, making conversation with the catering staff.

"How was it?" Andy whispered.

"Fine, I guess ... Andy, I'm so sorry about Milo."

"Thanks. Well, we'll talk about it later, my queen."

I could see Andy was upset. But, as always, his strength rose to the occasion.

"So, here's the plan," he said. "Scotty will walk down the satin path, carrying the cross and his Bible; then he'll stand under the arch and lay it on the pedestal. Next will be Trevor and Dean, who will stand to the right of the arch. When we hear the music play 'here comes the bride,' everyone will stand turn and watch the two of us walk the path. I will give your hand to Trevor, you will provide me with your bouquet of white roses, and Scotty will take it from there. But not until I have all the guests seated in those cute white chairs sitting in the sand. Sound okay to you, my queen?"

I nodded my approval, just as Derrick approached.

"Trevor, we may have a problem." The concerned look on his face sent chills spiraling through my body.

"What?" Trevor was trying to keep his cool.

"I just realized that I've met your Chief Armstrong before. He was at a Gang Meeting Task Force Seminar in Los Angeles about two years ago. I had a couple of drinks with him afterward in the hotel bar."

Andy couldn't help but overhear what Derrick said. "What the fuck! Are you serious?" he whispered. "Then he knows you're a cop! What the hell should we do?"

Derrick smiled as if nothing was wrong and put his hand on Andy's shoulder to calm him down. "I'm going to walk over to him and see if he remembers me. If he does, I'll just tell him the truth. That Monica and I have known each other for a long time, from our old school days. Malibu is a small place. Don't worry. I'll take care of it. So, Andy, when are you going to get this wedding rolling?"

Andy took a deep breath and smiled nervously. "Twenty to thirty minutes. Why?"

"I need to talk to Dean and explain the situation and then go greet the chief."

"Take all the time you need: I'm good at stalling," Andy said with a smile.

***

Derrick walked off and picked up two glasses of Champagne off the gold tray sitting on the table. He handed one to Dean. "We might have a problem, Dean. I've met Chief Armstrong before."

He glanced in Armstrong's direction. "Has he recognized you?"

"Not sure. How do you want to handle this?" Derrick patted Dean on the back, making sure he was facing with his back to where Armstrong and Flynn were standing.

"The chief isn't a stupid man. If he recognizes you, he'll warn his thugs that law enforcement is on the premises. I doubt they'll go through with their plans to get the cross, leaving us no alternative but to let them walk away after the wedding. We need them to steal the cross. At least we can arrest them on theft charges. Andy just told me that Flynn and Armstrong came into town yesterday. The same day Milo was murdered at the National Hotel. Maybe they're the killers. I don't know what Milo could have done to piss them off, if indeed it was them. If I could just arrest them on something tangible, like the cross. I could break them both."

"We're sticking out like a sore thumb with these earpieces. We need to pocket them. Where's your sidearm?"

Derrick subtly patted his side. "Think I'll take a little stroll over to the chief. It might deflate the situation sooner if I make the first move."

"Okay, Derrick. Be careful."

"Chief Armstrong?" Armstrong and Flynn turned around. "Do you remember me, sir?"

Armstrong studied Derrick's face. "I do remember you. Edwards, right?"

"Yes, sir. Derrick Edwards."

Armstrong gave Derrick a fake smile. "The Gang meeting in LA a couple of years ago. We had a few drinks at the bar. How you doing, son? You must be a detective by now."

"Yeah, still wearing the badge. Only now it's suits and ties every day." He smiled and turned his attention to Flynn. "And who is this lovely lady?"

"Excuse my manners, Derrick. This is Ms. Johnni Flynn. She owns a tavern in Ashbee Cove and is also friends with Trevor and Monica. We drove down together." He put his arm around her.

Derrick shook her hand. "Very pleased to meet you, Ms. Flynn," he said before turning his attention back to the chief. "Then you're still the chief in Ashbee Cove, sir?"

"Yep. I like the small-town feel. More comfortable for me as I'm getting older. Less crime to worry about."

"It sounds like your small town has had its share of murders lately. What's going on?"

An almost imperceptible look of shock passed over Armstrong's face, but he responded without a flinch. "You know how it is, Edwards. We've got a couple of ongoing investigations."

"Well, good luck, Chief. Nice seeing you again. It's been a pleasure, Ms. Flynn."

Flynn shrugged Armstrong's arm from around her shoulder. "Oh, this is just great. There's a cop here? This means there's probably a couple more roaming around. Now what?"

"My guys are already in place. I'll text them to take out Edwards first. I saw his weapon under his shirt. He won't have a chance to use it. Relax, this will still work. Just stick to the plan."

She shot him a look. "You better know what you're doing, asshole. I'm not going to prison." She walked off to get another glass of Champagne.

Shea Adams

Chapter 18

Andy looked at his watch. "Are you ready to do this?"

I glanced at Dean, who nodded slightly. I nudged my fiancé. "*Are* we ready, Doctor?"

He gave me a kiss on the cheek and whispered in my ear. "I love you."

"Then, let's do this, Doctor Bowen."

Andy tapped his Champagne glass. "Okay, dear friends and guests! Will you please take a seat in those white chairs on the beach. We are ready for a wedding!" He raised his glass as the guests began walking down to the area in front of the arch facing the Pacific Ocean.

Once everyone was seated, Andy motioned for the band to start playing.

One of the band members was an incredible singer. I realized when he started singing "All My Life" by K-CI & JOJO. Scotty walked down the satin walkway first, followed by Trevor and Dean. Andy looked at me.

"Okay, my queen, this is your magic moment." He kissed me on the cheek and handed me my wedding bouquet before putting my arm through his.

I looked into his eyes. "Thank you for this, Andy."

I caught a tear and a lump in this throat. Andy simply smiled, and we started walking towards my destiny.

Oh, my God. This really is happening ...

Halfway down the walk, the band began to play the "wedding march." All the guests stood to watch me walk down the satin runway. Slowly, Andy led me towards my waiting Prince. Trevor stepped forward, and Andy placed my hand in Trevor's hand. With tears in his eyes, he said, "Take care of her, my king."

Trevor nodded, and then we both turned to face Scotty.

Scotty placed his hand on the Bible and held up the Celtic cross.

"It is one of our life's richest surprises," he began, "when the accidental meeting of two souls joins them together as one and a relationship grows into a permanent bond of love. This meeting and this path that Trevor and Monica have chosen brings us together today, to witness their bond of love for each other. The circle in the center of this cross is a symbol, of the sun, the earth, and the universe. It is also a symbol of unity, in which two lives are joined as one in an unbroken circle. As is the circle of the cross, so is the circle of the ring."

As best man, Dean handed the ring that was given to Trevor by Scotty.

"Trevor, please place the ring on Monica's finger, as this ring will symbolize your unity and love."

What Trevor didn't know was that when Scotty found the antique emerald ring in Ireland, he also bought the matching emerald band, which he secretly gave to me. Andy was part of the surprise and had the ring in his pocket. He handed it to me, and the look on Trevor's face was priceless.

Scotty continued. "Monica, would you please place this ring on Trevor's finger, as this ring will symbolize your unity and love." Trevor looked at Scotty and smiled. "In as much as you two have come to your friends and guests and have declared your love and devotion to each other, I now greet you with all those present and declare you husband and wife. Trevor, you may kiss your bride."

And he did, to applause. I gazed up at him with pure love and adoration in my heart.

"Nicely played with the ring, Mrs. Bowen," he whispered.

The ceremony over, Andy and Dean escorted Scotty down the satin walkway, with Scotty still holding the cross. Trevor took my hand, and we followed the trio back up the satin path and onto the deck. The guests followed us as the band played another song, Bruno Mars' "Just the Way You Are."

Andy rushed up to me and threw his arms around me, crying. "Oh, my God! That was *so* beautiful! I can't believe you two are married. Just blows my freaking mind!" He pulled Trevor into the mix for a group hug. "I love you guys so much," he said through tears.

"Oh, stop it!" I begged. "You'll start me crying."

I walked up to Scotty and planted a kiss on the cheek. "Thank you, Scotty. Your words were beautiful."

Trevor came up and shook his hand. "Thank you, sir. The ceremony was amazing. And the ring was a total surprise!" He looked at it on his finger.

"You are both very welcome. It was my pleasure, I assure you. Now, what would you like me to do with the cross? Are we still going with our original plan or would you like me to have Andy put it back in the safe?"

"Yes, Scotty. You can display it on the table," I said. "I'll ask Andy to go inside and bring out the crimson cloth. Derrick will be nearby, keeping a close eye on Armstrong and Flynn. Please be careful. By no means are you to try and be a hero, Scotty. Understand?"

I walked over to Andy and asked him to go inside and get the cloth. He returned, handing it to Scotty, who placed it under the cross.

The guests were milling about the deck, enjoying the catered food and spirits. Some were gently dancing to the music; even people who were not invited to the wedding, but were nearby enjoying their time at the beach, joined in dancing on the sand, clapping for us. I smiled until I caught sight of our "special guests."

Armstrong and Flynn had made their way to the table where Scotty was sitting.

"That was a beautiful ceremony. They look very happy," Flynn said to Scotty.

"Thank you. I'm sure Monica and Trevor will live a long and happy life together." Scotty sipped a Scotch that one of the catering staff had brought him. The remaining crew was busy filling up Champagne glasses at other tables in preparation for the official toasting.

***

Armstrong and Flynn excused themselves from the table and moved to a corner on the deck. Armstrong discreetly turned towards the water and spoke into his cell phone.

"I want you to take out the guy standing next to the Champagne. He's wearing a beige shirt and a deep-brown tie. He's a cop and is packing. You know what to do next."

He disconnected the call and punched in another number. "Watch for my signal. As soon as we have the cross, open fire. Understand?" He turned to Flynn. "It's in place. We go on my signal, not before."

Flynn smiled.

***

Dean picked up a Champagne glass and prepared to speak to the guests. On cue from Andy, the music stopped.

"Will you all please come and get a drink so we can toast the bride and groom?"

Everyone shuffled over to the table and took a glass of Champagne as Trevor and I walked over to Dean, who snuggled in between us. Andy came to stand next to me, and Derrick flanked my husband. *Husband* ... Only now did the word hit home to me. *Oh, my God—I'm married!* A thrill went tingling up my spine and burst through my chest as I grinned stupidly. But I just couldn't help it.

Scotty joined Andy, leaving the cross on the table unattended, leaving Armstrong and Flynn to join the other guests near the table. I watched as they remained on the outside ring of guests.

Dean started his toast. "On behalf of Monica and Trevor, I would like to thank all of you for joining them on this special day. I have only known Monica a brief time but have known Trevor since our college days. He always had great taste in women then and obviously has better taste now." He turned to each of us and raised his glass. "May your life be filled with love."

Dean stopped talking.

Only then did I see what he saw: a red laser dot on Derrick's shirt. Dean tossed his glass on the table and lunged towards Derrick.

A soft *thump!* and Derrick wobbled. He put his hand up to his neck and collapsed, blood gushing from his wound.

Hearing the delayed gunshot sounds, people on the deck started screaming and scattering for cover.

I gasped a "No!" as Trevor grabbed me, forced me to the deck, covering me as we fell. A second shot thudded into something—or some*one*. I looked up to see Dean desperately scanning to see where the shots were coming from, still applying pressure to Derrick's wound.

"Trevor, are you two, ok? The shots are coming from that fishing boat a few yards offshore."

I heard the screams from those on the beach, and Dean yell above the panic, "Stay down!"

Andy had pushed Scotty to the deck, trying to cover him with his body. He yelled at me. "Monica! What should we do?"

I reached for his hand. "Stay down, Andy, stay down ... Trevor, are you hit?"

"No, but Derrick needs help fast."

"Andy, Call 911!"

He whipped out his cell. "Monica, there's no service! What the hell?!"

"Shit, someone's jammed the cell-phone signal. My gun is right near the door, in the drawer of the table. Can you get to it?"

Trevor looked at the slider. "I think so." He pushed over one of the tables nearby to give him some cover and scrambled to reach the table inside and take out my Glock. He slid it across the deck to me.

"I need to help Dean. Stay with Andy and Scotty."

He nodded, and when the gunshots suddenly stopped, he looked up to see what was happening, scanning to see if anyone else had been injured.

A groan came from the steps leading to the sand on the other side of the deck. Ivan. Before I could stop him, Trevor rushed to his side.

As he cried out, "Ivan's hit!" I scrambled over to join Dean and immediately helped him apply pressure to Derrick's gushing neck. I looked up to see Trevor take off his shirt, folding it to make a compress for Ivan.

"Ivan, keep the pressure on the wound, and you'll be okay; it looks like a flesh wound."

Trevor scrambled over to join Dean and me.

"Sorry, Trevor," Dean said. "We didn't expect an attack was coming from the ocean."

He nodded, then looked down at Derrick and made a move to help, grabbing a linen napkin, he put it on Derrick's neck.

He looked up at me and shook his head. "Sorry, Monica. He's gone."

Trevor now saw the blood soaking through the right side of Dean's pants. "Dean, you've been hit!"

"I know. I'll be fine. Where are Armstrong and Flynn?"

"Christ!" I exclaimed. I looked around the deck. The cross was no longer on the table. "It's gone!"

"And so are they," Trevor added.

"Go get those sons of bitches, Monica!" Dean cried. "They couldn't have gotten far."

Trevor patted Dean on the shoulder. "Hang in there, buddy." He looked at me.

We may only have been married five minutes, but I knew right away what was going through his head. "No way!" I said. "You're not going after them—I am."

"Mrs. Bowen. We'll go after them together. Doctor's orders."

"Andy!" I cried. "Get over here; I need your help!"

"Stay down, Scotty, yes?"

"I have no other plans, Andy. Go."

Andy crawled over to me. "What can I do?" Seeing all the blood, he added, "Oh, my God!"

Trevor took Andy's hands. "Dean needs pressure on this wound until help comes. You can do this, Andy. Use a napkin. Tie it around his leg. Anything to apply pressure, okay?"

Andy nodded. "I've got this."

I nodded to Andy, pulled back the slide on my gun, and looked at my husband. "Ready, Doc?"

"Yes, ma'am."

"Let's get these bastards."

We sprang up and ran, crouching, around the side of the bungalow to the front, where Armstrong had parked his car.

Several gunshots rang out from the top of the hill near the security gate to greet our arrival.

"Oh shit, Trevor, look!" I said, catching the masked gunman who had no doubt just killed the guard. I watched him push the button to open the gate, allowing Armstrong and Flynn to make their escape. "Come on!"

I fired two shots as we took off up the hill, watching the taillights on the car carrying Armstrong and Flynn. Two bullets *pinged* off the ground just as we dove for cover behind a large boulder.

"Okay, Doctor?" I asked panting.

"Okay, Mrs. Bowen?"

I popped my arm out and snapped off two shots in the direction of the shooter. *At least, I can give him something to think about.*

"Monica! I think I hear sirens!"

I listened ... "Yes, I hear them, too! The cavalry has arrived, thank God."

"Can't come soon enough." He smiled at me. "I hope we've got enough Champagne left."

This man! I grinned hugely. When you're being shot at, strange things go through your mind and out your mouth.

Another round of gunfire, then suddenly a loud explosion shook the ground beneath us. I gasped as I watched an ambulance veer over the cliff and crash on the beach below, bursting into flames.

I shrank back as more gunshots ricocheted off the rock, we were behind. "Shit! No help anytime soon."

Another explosion rocked us. Trevor peeked around our rock. "Another blast at the other end of the road!"

"To block any possibility of first responders helping us. Shit!"

"Hey ..."

I turned to where Trevor was gesturing to see Dean, limping towards us. Two shots *pinged* close to him, courtesy of the shooter at the gate. I snapped off another two rounds of my own, giving Dean enough time to reach us.

"What the fuck's going on?" Dean panted, his leg bleeding under the tourniquet Andy had wrapped around it.

"The shooter at the gate has us pinned down," I said. "More shooters at the top of the road, and I think the explosions we just heard blocked both ends of the road leading down to the Colony. There won't be help coming anytime soon."

"There are minor casualties; not sure if one of the waitresses will make it either. Everyone else seems to be okay, for now. I'm sorry about Derrick; he was a good man."

"How's the cell-phone signal?"

Dean shook his head. "Nothing!" Armstrong really planned this tight. His guys must have come in earlier to set up something to jam the signal."

"They made their escape with no problem and are long gone, already," I said.

Dean checked his gun clip.

"Look!" Trevor hissed. "Over there!"

"Christ, another shooter. He's headed for the bungalow! Trevor, we've got to get back there."

"You two go," Dean said. "I'll cover you."

"Thanks, buddy. Watch yourself."

"On three," I said.

We scrambled up and sprinted for the bungalow. A shot whistled past my ear before Dean returned a couple of rounds, giving us breathing space. *What the ...?* A caterer was flailing about like a headless chicken. "For God's sake!" I yelled at him. "Get back inside!"

We reached the garage entrance to the bungalow and took cover.

"He's going to kill everyone!" Trevor whispered hoarsely.

"Not if we can surprise him." We were now crouched down behind my Porsche Boxster. "No one else dies today, Doctor. There's a twelve-gauge shotgun in the entry closet. Do you know how to use a shotgun?"

"How hard can it be? Cock and shoot, right?"

"Yeah, pretty much. We'll both go inside; I only have a couple more shots in this clip, but extra clips are in a box on the top shelf of the closet."

Trevor nodded.

Carefully, I opened the back door, and we inched our way towards the entry closet. The reflection in the mirror on the wall sent a chill down my spine. The masked gunman coming out of nowhere was now standing on the deck, his gun pointed at Andy's head.

Shit!

"Where's the fucking cross, you fag!"

"Your asshole bosses took it, dear," I heard Andy reply. "It's not here; you can see that. Please just leave us alone."

Trevor looked at me. "Armstrong and Flynn don't have the cross?"

"I don't know. Here!" I handed Trevor the shotgun and jammed a fresh clip into my Glock, pulling back the slide. Good to go. *Time to get this asshole.*

"Wait, Monica. Why would they run if they didn't get the cross? Something isn't right."

"I don't give a shit about that damn cross. He's got a gun pointed at Andy's head. And he'll start killing people until he gets his answer."

Trevor nodded. We moved towards the glass slider out to the deck, me leading.

The shooter was, thankfully, facing away from us. He crossed over to Ivan, who looked like he had almost passed out—from loss of blood, no doubt.

"Tell me where the cross is now, or you die."

It was then that I placed the accent. *He's Irish!*

Ivan covered his head with his arms. "Please," he groaned. "I don't know where it is." The shooter put the gun to Ivan's head and pulled the trigger. The cowering guests began screaming.

"*Shut UP!*" He waved the gun around in the air. "You *all* die if I don't have the cross in my hands in *one* minute!"

"Trevor, we need to end this now!" I had a bead on the killer. I slipped out, Trevor beside me. One of the guests looked like she was about to say something as she lay cowed on the wooden planks now stained with blood. I put my fingers to my lips for her to be quiet.

"Drop your weapon, asshole!" I yelled.

On another day, I would have had him there and then, but Scotty was right behind him in my line of sight.

It was a hesitation I'd come to regret.

The shooter grabbed Andy, once again pointing his gun at his head. He turned around slowly.

"This man dies unless you give me the cross. Understand, bitch?" His weapon was cocked, I saw. Which meant the slightest movement of his finger could mean instant death for Andy.

Shit! Keep calm, I told myself. *I need to reason with him.* I took a deep breath. "Your fucking boss has the cross. It's gone. We don't have it."

The gunfire had stopped up the road. The sound of the waves crashing against the sand and the soft sobbing of those injured and scared were all we heard.

A sudden, lone gunshot rang out, echoing from the direction where Dean had been exchanging fire with the shooter at the gate. I glanced at Trevor. Dean only had a few bullets left in his clip. Besides, I knew, this last shot was rifle fire; it couldn't have come from Dean's pistol gun. Dean was likely dead.

"Monica?" Trevor, too, had somehow come to the same conclusion. Dismay spread across his face and now anger. My heart went out to him, but I still had to save Andy.

"Look, there's nowhere to go; the road is destroyed. The police will hunt you down and catch you in no time. And it's gone. The cross is gone. So, once again, drop that gun, and let's have no one else die today."

The gunman pulled at his mask removing it, throwing it aside.

"Mickey Ryan, what the fuck are you doing?!" Trevor screamed.

"Ryan, wait. We don't have it. Armstrong and Flynn have it," I pleaded, trying to distract him away from his target: Andy's head.

"Not without the cross. I'm a dead man if I don't get it." He pressed the gun harder against Andy's skull.

Trevor moved and walked towards the gunman. "Trevor, wait!" He paused for a second when he caught me pointing out to the ocean. He, too, now saw the fishing boat had returned, just offshore. He turned back to Ryan. "You don't have to do this."

"You don't understand, Dr. Bowen. I helped kill that family. They sent me to get the cross or they would frame me, say it was only me who killed them. But, I didn't. I swear!

"Who killed them, Ryan?" Trevor asked, his shotgun still pointed at Ryan now no more than a foot away.

"Ryan, please," I said. "Give it up or you're a dead man either way. I kill you or Armstrong does. I don't give a fuck who pulls the trigger, but your bosses have the cross—they're setting you up, Ryan."

I saw that moment. That instant where the doubt creeps in and the alternative is suddenly on the table.

"Slowly drop that weapon," I continued, my voice stern but calm, "and back away."

I heard the familiar sound of a slide being pulled back on a handgun. I turned and saw a second gunman with his gun pointed at the two us.

A deep voice came from behind the mask. "Lay down your weapons, now!" Again, an Irish accent.

Before I could respond, there was a lone shot. But from where ...?

As if in slow motion, the gunman fell to the ground. Dean was leaning against the bungalow's wall, bleeding from his chest.

But alive!

He dropped his weapon and collapsed.

"Go to him, Trevor," I said and looked back at the gunman standing over Andy. "Don't do it!" I said, my voice as controlled as possible.

Andy looked at me, his face calm.

Like he knows he's going to die. Oh, God!

I knew I was the better marksman, and I was out of options. I winked at Andy. He knew what I meant and winked back.

"Okay, listen, Ryan," I said. "How about ..." I pulled the trigger, just as I saw Andy curl up into a ball, breaking away from the shooter.

Blood and brain matter splattered into the air as Ryan's body sank to the deck—dead.

I ran to Andy and crouched down. "It's okay, Andy. He's dead. You did good!"

He looked up at me with tears rolling down his face. "I'm okay, my queen. Go check on Trevor and Dean. I'll help the others and Scotty."

Trevor was now standing. Dean slumped at his feet.

"He's gone, Monica. Dean is dead."

He stood, pulling me to his chest. It was like I could feel his pain flood through my body. "I'm so sorry, Trevor."

"How many others ...?" Trevor looked down at Dean's lifeless body.

I tried to catch my breath. "I'm not sure."

Trevor looked up at a police helicopter now hovering over the bloody scene. "Why couldn't they have gotten here earlier, Monica?"

"They're here now, and the rest of us are safe." I held onto him as tightly as I could.

Another scream.

"Monicaaaa! Laaaseeer!" Andy was frantically yelling at me.

What?

I looked down at the red dot on my chest. Before I could react, Trevor grabbed hold of my shoulders and pushed me away. I stumbled and collapsed. I looked up to see the bullet thud into his chest. Blood suddenly gushed as he crumpled to the ground.

For a moment, I was frozen. A primal scream erupted from deep inside me. "NO!!!!" I scuttled over to him, my nails digging into the wood as I frantically tried to get purchase.

"Trevor!!" I looked into his fluttering eyes, cradled his head in my arms. "Please God ... Please, don't let him die."

The fluttering eased, and he seemed serene when his eyes met mine.

A quiet whisper, "I love you, Mrs. Bowen. I ... I'm ... sorry." He exhaled his last breath on this earth.

"*Nooooo!!!!*" My wail must have carried across the whole Colony. But there were no tears. Not yet, not here, not now. Just a heat, a fire, raging white-hot inside of me. I lay Trevor's sweet head down and picked up my Glock, got up, and charged past Andy and Scotty, both in shock at what just happened.

I flew towards the boat at a speed I never knew I had. Rage burned in my soul. I could feel it, literally burning up and through my eyes. And I would unleash hell on that *murdering BASTARD* standing on the deck of the boat.

I saw him raise the rifle. I knew my death was imminent, but I didn't care. "You're a dead man!"

A bullet whistled past me. How it missed, I don't know. I screamed a primal rage of grief and revenge as I ran through the breaking waves towards the boat. "*You killed him! You killed him!!*" I raised my Glock and emptied it at the man who'd destroyed my life.

He jerked and shuddered as each and every shot hit him. The last one spun him on the deck of the boat before he plunged into the water.

I came to a breathless halt and sank, crawling my way back onto the sand, burying my face in my hands as I dropped the gun.

Some moments later, I don't know how many, I registered a soft touch on my shoulder. I looked up through my frazzled hair and tears to see Andy kneeling beside me.

"A-Andy ... h-he's gone ... Trevor's g-gone ... They killed him. That bullet was meant for me! *Me!* Not Trevor. Why, Andy? Why did he push me?"

He wrapped me in his arms. "Oh, my queen. You know why: he loved you."

I sobbed ragged breaths that wracked me. I wanted to die.

"We need to go back, now," Andy said softly. "Say goodbye to Trevor, yes?"

"Yes," I sobbed.

He helped me up from the sand and guided my shaking body back to the deck.

Troopers were on the ground now, and on the deck helping the victims. I turned when I heard a thunderous explosion. The boat debris scattered across the blue Pacific.

I walked over to Trevor's lifeless body, now covered with a blue plastic sheet, and sat down; I pulled the cover back to expose his sweet face, and I cradled my husband once again in my arms. Gently, I placed a last kiss on his lips.

"I love you, Trevor Bowen, forever. I got him, sweetie. I got him ... And Armstrong and that Flynn bitch will rot in jail. I'll see to it ... I'll do it, Trevor. I'll do it. I'll get the killers and close the case. Armstrong and Flynn will never hurt anyone else again. Can you hear me ...?"

I don't know how long I stayed there, cradling and rocking my husband in my arms.

But it wasn't long enough.

Epilogue

Andy and Monica are sitting on the deck some days later, recalling the funeral, trying to come to terms with the tragedy. They sit, taking in the peace of the ocean that will, eventually, calm their souls. In the meantime, they have each other.

Monica will heal ... in time. But will she ever love again?

Follow Monica Wade on her next adventure. Her job is to catch the bad guys. And she never fails. No matter what the cost.

THE END

Shea Adams

Afterword and thanks

Writing is a passion that lets loose the creative mind—sometimes in ways that give pause to friends and family, thinking that this can't really be coming from my daughter, my mother, my grandmother, my sister, or my friend ... can it?

I owe a lot of people some heartfelt thanks. First, and foremost, thank you, dear reader, for purchasing this book and joining Monica on her journey. I've published this novel independently, which means it's wonderful readers like you that have the power to make or break its success. If you've enjoyed it, may I ask you to quickly drop by Amazon and/or Goodreads and leave a quick review? Would-be readers read reviews, or at least the book's rating, so even a single line to say why you liked The Ashbee Cover Murders would be great. Thanks!

I'd like to give a special thank you to Dean, who has been relentless in his encouragement for me to keep being creative. To Gayleen, who gave me character input and made me laugh. To my editor, Jay: you made me a better writer with your strong criticism, yet built me up at the same time. I thank you for slapping my hands with a (soft) ruler.

I hope you enjoyed the ride. I like Monica Wade and consider her a friend, at least in my mind. She has been a joy and, at times, a confusing fiction character to write! But Monica is not done ... yet. Look out for *The Perfect Stranger* and *The Art of Murder: The Shadow Man*—out spring 2021—and the forthcoming *Who Killed Rosemary Bud?*

LOVE and HUGS to all,

Shea Adams

About Shea Adams

Born in Sayre, Oklahoma and now residing in Northern California, Shea Adams loved to write from a young age, whether song lyrics, poetry, or short stories. After many years of collecting her works, Shea decided it was time to try her hand at being a published author, and so sat down one day, pulled out her manuscripts, and found she had a love for writing mysteries. And thus, Monica Wade, PI, began her casebook series.

Part detective mystery, part romance, Shea's books feature a strong female protagonist who takes the lead in dealing with danger, thieves, and murderers. The characters are written to display warmth and wit so readers enjoy spending time with them. For those that enjoy such writers as J.D. Robb, Tracy Brogan, Patricia Bradley, and Lynette Eason and TV shows like the classic Hart to Hart and Remington Steele, Shea Adams will not disappoint.

Her first novel, *The Ashbee Cove Murders*, introduces Monica Wade PI and her best friend and support, the flamboyant Andy Weston. The sequels, *The Perfect Stranger* and *The Art of Murder*, find Monica on unexpected adventures as she searches for direction in her life. *Who Killed Rosemary Bud?*, due to be released in 2021, again features the intrepid detecting duo, showcasing Shea Adams's talent as a mystery writer on the rise.

Find Shea at her **author page**

www.sheaadamsauthor.com

On **Facebook**

www.facebook.com/sheaadams.author

Find Shea's books on **Amazon.com**

- search for "Shea Adams" in the books category

Coming 2021 in the *Monica Wade – Private Investigator* series

- spring 2021: *The Perfect Stranger*
- summer 2021: *The Art of Murder: The Shadow Man*
- fall 2021: *Who Killed Rosemary Bud?*

Printed in Great Britain
by Amazon